CW00854476

Azzurra;

The Tale of the Dead Princess

Briony McMahon

Azzurra; The Tale of the Dead Princess

Copyright © 2021 by Briony McMahon

First edition

ISBN: 9798460885459

Contents

V   Continued in:

Dedicated

To

...

All the introverts, adventure lovers and fairy-tale

dreamers.

Thank you,

for choosing my world,

to get lost in.

...

Azzurra; The Tale of the Dead Princess

I'm going to tell you a story that's never been told before,

But one, you know well.

A tale of bravery immersed in a pool of evil and deception.

Wrapped in a world of magic and mystery,

Encased in a love story with an unwritten ending

A simple fairy tale,

Disguised by many layers of imagination.

Yours and mine

Welcome to Azzurra

Part One

We are all tied through the generations,

and in that bond, we will never be lost,

never forgotten and always, always

together.

Location: The Pink Mountains, Training Ground.

The blood dripped onto the crisp white snow at my feet.

I felt the warmth on my skin as I wiped the rest of the

thick red liquid from my nose. Nook stared at me,

horrified. He was the same age as me, almost exactly,

only minutes between us, and he was Chief Eire's only

blood child. The future Chief of the Camp. He was swift, precise with his attacks. He'd gone easy on me, and still, he'd landed a punch. I was no child of the Pink Mountains, and it was becoming abundantly more apparent as we aged. Nook let out a low whistle that stopped the rest of the kids mid-training. They all turned to look; focused in on the blood still dripping from my nose. I was met with the usual groans and murmurs of the other children at having to stop because of me. They all grabbed their gear and ran fast across the tundra of white back towards the camp. In the distance, racing towards us at the smell of blood, its thumping footsteps grew louder and louder as it narrowed in on us. Nook turned back to see I hadn't moved. He ran back, grabbed my hand, and tried to pull me after him, but it was too late. We both stood frozen in the field of white with nowhere to hide. Our breath clouded in front of us as the brown and white skin of the four-legged beast came into view. Its devilish black eyes locked onto me. Sprinted towards me at unbelievable speeds. Its large padded wolfish paws bouncing with ease off the snow floor. Nook held my hand tighter as it smiled, a big fanged and toothy grin. A shriek filled our ears, so loud it could have broken every window in The Sovereign City. As the beast prepared for his final pounce, jaw ready to snap down over me, claws razor-sharp, I realised the shriek was coming from me.

I screamed myself, silent as the beast leapt into the air, casting a shadow down over our shaking bodies. Still holding Nook's hand, I covered my face with my arms, and suddenly I felt a sensation I'd never felt before. It lasted only a second, and when it was over, I dropped my arms and opened my eyes to see Nook staring back at me with confusion and disbelief. 'Aveline? How did you do that?' Nook's mouth dropped ajar. I looked around to see the beast nowhere in sight. Instead of the snowy abyss that should've been our grave, we were on the edge of the dense forest not far away. Nook grabbed my hand, unwrapped it from the black tape we used for training to protect ourselves from injury, and turned it over to see my palm. We both looked to see a fading blue circle; it was dark, almost liquid, moving as if it were a part of me.

I met Nook's eye, afraid. 'What does it mean?' I closed my hand tight, willing it to go away.

'I, I'm not sure. I've never seen one like that before….' Nook drifted off, distracted by something behind me. I turned to see what was so much more important and saw a creature I'd never seen before. Never heard of. I looked closely at the faint purple tint of its skin, its slightly pointed ears and tiny nose. Even the rock-solid looking hair that ran backwards down its shoulder blades. I stepped after Nook towards it, intrigued. He was just as taken aback.

'What is it?' I whispered without looking away from the sleeping creature, nestled amongst the snow.

'I think it's a… *faery*,' he replied. I stepped closer again. 'Careful. They're dangerous.' He touched my arm to stop me. I looked back, confused at the delicate creature asleep before us. 'Things like her, they're the reason we're to keep away from the Blue Forest.' He continued. 'I've never seen one up close before, though.' His eyes drifted back. Enamoured by the creature.

Enchanted perhaps. 'I wonder what its name is…' he stepped closer still.

Butternut. I heard a lyrical voice in my head. I turned to Nook; he hadn't heard it.

'Nook.' I whispered so as not to wake the creature. He ignored me. It was like he couldn't hear me.

Then from a distance, the snow beast's snarl echoed towards us; we both turned; Nook snapped from his trance and hurriedly crept back to the tree line to see the beast pacing around my blood drops still on the snow. It was confused, angry. 'It's not leaving.' I said, looking past the beast to where our camp lay in the distance, hidden beneath the snow. Nook was about to reply when black smoke shot through the sky and exploded through the clouds casting a shadow so large it would be seen throughout Azzurra. We both watched as darkness fell.

We traced it back to its origin, The Sovereign City Palace. 'Something bad has happened.' I looked to Nook, worried. I could see in his head he was already working on a plan to get past the beast. 'You can't!' I pushed him, snapping him out of his ridiculous train of thought. 'You know the rules. We don't kill for sport, just for survival.'

'We have to do something – '

'Not *that*.' As I spoke, the snow beast took off back in the direction it came from. The growing darkness had spooked it. Nook looked relieved but tried to hide it; this made me smile. I looked back to where the faery had been. 'She's gone.' I frowned.

Nook looked back too. 'She shouldn't have been this far out anyway. We should tell the Chief.'

'She looked harmless.' I pointed out.

'They all do. That's what's so scary about faeries. They're easy to underestimate and hard to say no to.' He put a hand on my shoulder. 'Couldn't you feel its pull?'

'Like it was drawing you in?'

Nook nodded. I nodded back, but I hadn't felt it, not like he had.

We crossed the blood drops that still glinted on the snow, Nook purposefully kicking snow over them to hide them. The camp wasn't far now, a few minutes walk, but Nook stopped. I turned back, the look on his face told me everything, he wanted to apologise. 'It's okay. I should've blocked.' I smiled back at him.

'I should've stopped myself.'

'If you had, the Chief would've been disappointed. You can't afford to hesitate.' I replied, knowing it was true, and it had been my fault. I wasn't good enough. No matter how hard I trained. I would never have the speed or endurance of the rest of Chief Eire's people. It wasn't in my blood.

'Don't think like that. You just need a bit more training. No one else has any doubts that you belong here.' Nook put his hand on my shoulder reassuringly. It was scary how well we knew each other sometimes. Like we could read each other's thoughts. We even looked similar, or maybe we'd just morphed over time, growing more and more alike.

'Are you kidding? All they do is complain that I hold them back.'

'Come on, mum and the Chief will be worried.' He put his arm around my shoulders, and we shuffled through the snow towards camp.

'The Chief should just tell them I don't belong here. Then they wouldn't expect so much of me….' I could feel a tear threatening the back of my eye. Nook tightened his arm around me.

'How are you ever going to improve if no one believes you can be better?'

Location: Pink Mountains, Chief Eire's Camp

The Camp wasn't exactly hidden, but it was a lot easier

to find if you knew where the entrance was. A set of iced

stairs leading down into the snow, approximately one

mile from the Southern Forest line, five and a half miles

from The Sovereign City wall, you could just see the

Palace tower in the skyline, twenty miles from the border of the Arid, Chief Keahi's land and fifteen miles from the border of Salt Glass City's magical underwater paradise. That was how it had always been told to me. Names of places I had never been to. Would never see. Could only imagine. There were rules to live by, necessary to survive in the land of the Pink Mountains, then there were hard rules set by Chief Eire. For me, that meant never leave the campground. For everyone else, it was don't stay out after dark alone, don't enter the Blue Forrest and don't break the treaties between the lands. I followed behind Nook as we entered the Camp. We walked the corridors built of ice blocks and snow; there wasn't a soul in sight until we reached the grub hub, the large room where we all ate. It was lined with long tables and benches. Usually, it was half full as people came in and out at all times of day between training and school to eat but not this time. This time when we entered, the grub hub was full. So full there weren't even enough seats for everyone. Chief Eire stood at the front of the room, beside her, Eos, Nook's mum. We slipped through the open door and immediately caught The Chief's eye. She beckoned us forward. We moved quickly through the crowd, all eyes on us, everyone waiting to hear the news. The Chief embraced us both warmly, glad we were okay. This wasn't unusual; I was always treated with love and kindness as if I were her own. What was different this time was she didn't let go of me again. She kept a hand on my shoulder, her arm around me as she addressed the room. While Nook knelt at her side, as I should have been, he looked at me questioningly. He had noticed, too; he knew I didn't know why when I looked back at him. Chief Eire squeezed my shoulder as she explained the Sovereign King had passed. 'It's a dark day for Azzurra. The King has reigned over the Sovereign City for almost four decades. He brought peace between the lands, allowed free trade, and allowed the lands to rule independently. He protected us from the Blue Forrest and kept the Moon Whisperers at bay. I fear now we will face a time of uncertainty. Possibly even the threat of war.' She tried her best to keep her voice steady, but there was fear in the room, growing panic. She looked to Eos, who nodded back; she should continue. Sugar-coating the truth would help no one. 'There is already talk that the King's brother, Lord Ellis, will take rule.'

Gasps and murmurs fill the room at the mention of his name from the older members of the camp. The children sat confused; Lord Ellis wasn't a name we'd ever heard before. This was when Eska piped up from the middle of the room. He was one of my favourite beings. He was born in the Forré, a small hidden land on the outskirts of The Sovereign City. He was covered in white fur. Some of which flopped down between his furry pointed ears on top of his head. He had mousy eyes that sat above an almost human-shaped nose. His face was shaped by the extending fur on his cheeks, where his hidden whiskers twitched occasionally. He was the same height as me, but I didn't know how old he was. The Forré don't age as we do. He could be twelve like Nook and me, or he could be as old as the Chief. I'd never dared ask. He spoke as if he were older as if he knew things we couldn't possibly.

'The rules the King put in place still stand. Lord Ellis has no right to the throne. The treaties still apply; every land must vote.' Eska explained to the room but aimed at Chief Eire.

'While this is true, the rules came with clauses. Clauses, we all accepted and signed. One of which was if the ruling party's death was anything other than natural causes. The vote to decide the next leader would be held in limbo until the culprit was found and duly punished. Until this time, the ruling party would assign a stand-in.'

'King Petri was murdered?' The words fell from Eska's mouth before he knew what was happening.

'It appears so. As it stands, The King was poisoned, killed in his sleep.' Chief Eire explained, this was shocking news to everyone, including Eos. She looked to Chief Eire, gobsmacked. Chief Eire hadn't told her. She turned to Eos, spoke so the room couldn't hear, only I because I stood between them, Chief Eire's arm still around me. 'It was confidential, shared only between the rulers of the lands.' Chief Eire looked sorry but not enough that she regretted it. Eos nodded understanding.

Nook got to his feet to address the Chief. 'Surely, Lady Alillia would take King Petri's place?' He asked, confused. Chief Eire stroked down his face as she spoke to him,

'They don't have the same rules as we do, son. Any blood relative can stand interim for their leader, not just their child.' She pushed down on his shoulder for him to return to one knee at her side, he did without argument. 'We are unfortunately standing in the unknown; we must prepare for the worst.' She finished with a solemn expression and gestured for everyone to leave. Slowly,

everyone started to get to their feet and return to their
normal, daily routine. Chief Eire pulled Nook to his feet
slowly with one arm and placed us next to each other.
She looked concerned, more so than I'd ever seen her. I
looked at Nook; he thought the same.

'What's wrong, mum?'

She held us each by the shoulder, sandwiching us
together. 'We knew there was a possibility this day
would come.' She glanced to Eos as she spoke. I looked
too; she didn't look pleased at all. 'Aveline, sweet girl.'

'Do I have to leave?' The question blurted out
without my consent, taking them all by surprise,
especially Nook.

It was Eos that broke the silence with words that
should've crushed my very soul, 'not yet' but they
didn't. Even Eos's stern tone didn't upset me. I was at

peace with the idea that the only family I'd ever known was prepared to throw me out into a world I'd never seen to save themselves.

'Mum?!' Nook exclaimed, completely beside himself at the thought. Chief Eire was filled with sorrow, but she knew she had a duty to protect her people. So, did I.

'You were always ahead of the game, you know that?' She bent down, so she was eye level with me. 'Somehow, you always knew the way the world worked without being told.'

'Who am I?' My voice cracked with emotion; I hadn't expected it to. I had forgotten how much the question meant to me and forced myself to forget how important that answer was.

'You, sweet girl, are a spark in a world scorched to ashes.' She stared at me long and hard. There was a flash of terror in the back of her eye that she couldn't hide. She hadn't meant the words as a compliment. Tears started to form in my eyes, emotion welled in my throat. Her words had hurt me. Hurt me more than Eos telling me I was little more than collateral damage. I wished that she hadn't answered me. I wished that she had continued to lie and ignore me as she had done every other time I had asked. I wasn't ready for the truth, and looking at Nook, he wasn't either.

'Mum, what are you talking about? Aveline is one of us. You always said- '

'She lied, Nook.' I found my voice. Strong. Certain. The tears had dried before they could fall. Nook grabbed my hand. Held it tight. I met his eye. As always, his face said everything. *I'll never leave you.* I smiled, small, just at the corners of my mouth, just big enough for him to see. Chief Eire straightened up.

'Go get cleaned up and join the other children for class.' Eos told us. Chief Eire nodded, gestured for us to go, and we did. Walked out, hand in hand, their stares burning holes in our backs. They knew more than they were telling, but I was too afraid to push for more. I felt Nook was the same.

We didn't join the other children. Something had changed; we both knew it. We went to my room. We were the only two children in the camp that had our own rooms. All the others slept in groups of eight once they turned five and started training. A small fire burned in my room; my clothes hung around it, drying. We both shed our outer layers, our fluffy boots, thick trousers, and long jackets. We sat on my bed, staring at the wall in our thermals. 'We didn't tell the Chief about what happened. When the beast came.' I told Nook, suddenly remembering the impossible thing that had happened only an hour ago. It seemed so small now. I sat forward then. 'Do you think she'd be surprised?'

Nook didn't follow. Not at first. Then he understood. Maybe the Chief knew I came from the bloodline of the Architects, the ones that built Azzurra. The ones that created the Scions, like the one that had appeared on my hand.

'She has no reason to keep that from you if she does.' He replied reassuringly. 'Scions aren't forbidden anymore, not under the King's rule. He made Azzurra safe for all.' He continued. I tucked my knees into my chest, huddled up small.

'The King's not here anymore…' he felt my fear at the thought. We sat in silence, watching the flames flicker back and forth. Chief Eire's news had rattled us. Until now, we had both lived in a lie. We had awoken to the truth that this would not be the place where I grew old. That I would not forever be his sister. That I would not have the chance to become Chief. I was lost in limbo, waiting to be claimed. Then, suddenly, the ceiling started to shake. Snow dust fell above us. Through the wall, we heard shouts, panic ensuing. The ceiling shook harder. We were both covered in a thin layer of snow dusting now. Confused as each other, we leapt from the bed and rushed to the door. I swung it open to see members of the camp sprinting down the hallways. They grabbed weapons, fighting gear, shouted at each other through the walls. I turned to Nook. 'We're under attack!' Our eyes shot wide with fear.

'Quick. C'mon!' he tugged at my arm to drag me back into the room. We hurriedly shoved our boots back on and grabbed our coats. There was no time for our outer protective layers. Nook threw the door open, and we leapt into the chaos. He held my hand as he guided us through the pounding footsteps and swinging knives. I dodged and ducked, jabbing elbows as we manoeuvred through the hallway.

'NOOK! NOOK!' Eos's voice rang through the crowd. Nook stopped abruptly. I crashed into the back of him, and we both hit the floor. Eos's hands were on me then, hauled me to my feet. Nook, already upright again. She half carried; half dragged me to Chief Eire's

Chambers, a second level underground. Nook hot on our heels.

Eos shut the door behind us, Nook locked it. 'What is going on?!' he demanded.

'Thank god… Aveline' Chief Eire breathed. Eos pushed me lightly towards the Chief and walked to block the door. I was short of breath, confused, scared, and wanting nothing more than for Chief Eire to wrap her arms around me and tell me everything was going to be okay. She didn't. She pulled a thick, pencil-sized object wrapped in silk from her pocket and held it out to me. It was purple and orange and shimmered, even without light. 'This is an illustrator. It was given to you when you were born… I thought we'd have more time.' Chief Eire explained. I reached out for it, the silk soft on my skin. I could see now; the illustrator was made from dragon scales.

'What does it do?' I asked, but the ceiling shook again; the shouts from upstairs echoed down.

'They're coming. We need to show our faces. Call a cease-fire.' Eos told Chief Eire. 'She can't be here.'

'I know.' Chief Eire spoke sternly. The ceiling shook again harder.

'Eire!'

Chief Eire looked unsure for the first time in my whole life. She grabbed me by the shoulders, held me tight. 'I will always love you, but I can't protect you from what's coming….' Her hand traced my arm from my shoulder to my palm where she held my hand; her thumb stroked my palm where the blue circle had appeared. I met her eye then. She knew. 'Be careful who you trust.'

She folded my hand up and kissed it before she hurried across the room. She threw a heavy tapestry to the side to reveal a ladder and beckoned me up. I shook my head. I couldn't.

'Where does it go?' I questioned.

'To the surface, near the Western Forest, there's a door to the smuggler's tunnels not far. Trust yourself. You'll find your way.' She reached forward and grabbed my arm, thrust me towards the ascending steps.

'Mum, are you insane?' Nook shouted. Eos's hand on his shoulder, holding him back.

'This is not up for discussion.' She hurried me up the steps. I went reluctantly. The metal, cold on my hands. Eos continued to hold Nook back as I disappeared up the narrow, mysterious passageway.

'No! Aveline!' Nook's shouts ended in a muffle.

I pushed through the thinly covered opening the other end and found myself on the edge of the campgrounds. The cold hit me in a flurry of icy winds. CSC soldiers from The Sovereign City were swarming the camp. I clambered out onto the snow, the illustrator tight in my hand, and I ran. As fast as I could. The snow was heavy, thick, my feet were starting to lag. I tripped, landing face-first in the snow. I looked back; Chief Eire had made it to the surface. She was confronting one of the soldiers. I felt hands on me then. I looked back to see Nook. He grabbed my coat and lifted me to my feet.

'What are you doing!' I gasped as he pulled me forward.

'Escaping with you!' He took off into a run, dragging me with him. I followed him blindly towards the Western Forest line. We darted through the trees until we reached a small clearing. Nook looked around as if trying to remember.

'Nook your parents!' I grabbed his arm to get his attention.

'They'll be fine.' He said sternly. He'd never spoken to me like that before. I didn't dare argue. 'This way.' His face, soft again. He ran to the most giant tree on the edge of the clearing and started kicking snow around. I watched, keeping one eye on the forest for the soldiers that were surely following us when I heard his boot connect with metal. I watched as he lifted a metal trap door open to reveal an underground stairway. He held his hand out to me; I didn't hesitate.

The only sound was our breathing. Shallow. I could hear my heart beating in my ears as we descended and pulled the trap door shut behind us. We were alone.

Armed with a single dagger and a mysterious dragon scaled pencil, we took our first steps into the darkness.

Part Two

The secrets you can uncover when

you are unexpected are the rarest

and most valuable of all

Location: Smuggler Tunnels.

'What is this place?' I asked as I fumbled to go down the last few steps.

'Smuggler tunnels. They were used in the old days by the Moon Whisperer's to smuggle stolen goods back to their ships and hideouts.' Nook explained as we started through the darkness. A few metres in and a light flicked on, on the wall beside us. As we continued, another and another. The one before turning off again.

'They came through the Pink Mountains?' I queried, in disbelief, that they would allow anyone to cross their land.

'The elder's said it was a different time. That the Moon Whisperers' were close to taking power.' Nook explained. 'They lied and traded their way into the pockets of the rulers until the people caught on and chased them out to the seas.' He breathed a big sigh of relief, and we walked in silence for a while after that.

I glanced at him a few times, building up the nerve to say, 'You didn't have to do that.'

'These are cool motion sensors. We should get these for camp.' He looked back into the darkness behind us.

'Nook?'

'Aveline.' We stopped in the glow of the only light. arkness on either side of us. 'You're my best friend –'

'And you're mine. I don't want you to get hurt because of me. You heard the Chief, I'm the spark that's going to destroy the world!'

'Or save it!'

'That's not what she said-'

'Well, it's what I'm saying. You're special, Aveline. Not because you're a Scion but because you never give up. Even when you're hopeless and can't keep up with everyone else. You never gave up. So, I'm *never* giving up on you.' Nook didn't often give out compliments, but they were nothing short of memorable when he did. I couldn't help but smile; part of me, nothing more than relieved I would never be alone.

'Well, don't look too happy. Someone's got to keep you alive out here…' Nook laughed. We turned to keep going; as we did, Nook knocked my arm, and the illustrator fell from its silk wrapping. With a gasp, I fumbled to grab it before it hit the floor. I caught it just in time, but as I did, I felt a sudden warmth shoot through me. The scales connected with my skin, and an orange liquid circle appeared on my palm in the same place as the blue one had. I couldn't breathe. I grabbed for Nook, caught his coat. My fingers wrapped around the soft fur as I struggled to catch my breath. I couldn't hear properly. Nook's mumbled words of worry came through blurred, my vision started to go. Darkness crept around my eye line. Then all of a sudden, I could see a street. Feel the cool breeze of the night on my skin and see the stars in the sky. It wasn't possible. I could still feel Nook's coat between my fingers, feel his hands on my shoulders and hear his voice muffled in the back of my head.

The street had cobbled stones, large street lanterns lighting the way. A door came into view, old, wooden, arched with a flower painted on it. 'Aveline! Aveline, what's wrong!' Nook's voice was getting louder, clearer. Then the old door opened, a girl, a teenager, was on the other side. She looked just like me but older, but it made no sense. Behind her was cold shimmering glass, not a warm, inviting home. In her hand was the illustrator. The same one I was holding now. 'AVELINE!' Nook's voice broke through, the door faded away, the older me too, but as she did, I could swear she looked right at me. As if she could see me. I sucked in a deep breath as I fell back into the tunnel, taking Nook down with me. He held me tight. Stroked my hair as I fought to catch my breath. 'What happened?!' He wrapped his arms tighter around me.

'I, I don't know...' I looked to the illustrator in my hand, behind it, the circle on my palm still shimmered, but now it was purple. It slowly faded. 'I saw something.' We both sat up; I wrapped the illustrator quickly back in its silk and tucked it safely away in my boot. 'A vision, I think.'

'Of the future?' Nook shuffled around on his knees to sit in front of me. I nodded slowly. 'I've never heard of a Scion having more than one Aura….'

'Then, why do I? What am I, Nook?' I asked, afraid. Nook had no answer. He dug around in his coat pocket and pulled out the black training tape. 'What are you doing?'

'We can't risk anyone else seeing your Scion Aura. Not if it changes.' He started to wrap my hand and wrist. 'Chief Eire kept you safe your whole life for a reason. If this is it, then we need to keep protecting it.'

I nodded in agreement; that made sense. Then something dawned on me. 'What if they already know?'

Nook looked back at me, confused as he finished securing the tape.

'They didn't attack our home for no reason. Not so soon after King Petri's death... they were there for *me*.'

Nook's expression finished the sentence, *and they'll keep coming.* He took my hand and pulled me to my feet. We had to keep moving.

We'd walked for half an hour when we came to a junction. The tunnel split into five; we stood at the edge of the tunnel that led back to the Pink Mountains and looked down the identical passages in front of us. 'Which way?' Nook asked. I shook my head. 'The Sovereign City is North, so it must be that one.' He pointed straight ahead of us. 'Salt Glass City is East.' He pointed to the tunnel on our right. 'The Arid.' He pointed left towards Chief Keahi's land.

'So, where does the fifth one go?' I asked, pointing to the only remaining tunnel.

'The unclaimed maybe?' He shrugged. I looked back at him, confused. 'Oh, right. Umm… the Unclaimed is a piece of land just past The Sovereign City. Mum said they couldn't decide who owned the land when they made the treaties, so they said no one could have it.'

Nook explained, a flash of guilt on his face. We both realised there were probably many stories I'd missed on the journeys to and from the Pink Mountains.

'Okay, so…' I sighed, looking between the passageways.

'Chief Keahi has always been an ally.' Nook took a step to the left.

'No.' I grabbed his arm. 'They'll know that. That could be the first place they look for me.'

'Okay, well… in your vision, you saw an old wooden door on a cobbled street, right?' He asked; I nodded in response. 'Well, The Sovereign City's the only place with cobbled streets.' He shrugged and took a step towards the tunnel opposite. I didn't follow. 'Aveline?' 'I think we should go this way….' I gestured to the tunnel leading to Salt Glass City. Nook looked back, confused. 'When I stepped out of the door in the vision, I think I came from Salt Glass City. Maybe that's where we'll find help?'

'I don't know; we don't have any supporters there. The Salt Glass Queen always had loyalty to the Sovereigns in the City….'

'Chief Eire said to trust myself. I had that vision for a reason.' I argued back softly. Nook wasn't convinced. He thought for a moment. Then reluctantly nodded.

'Okay, but the first sign of trouble and we bolt, deal?' He extended his hand to me. I shook it firmly.

'Deal.'

We came to the end of the tunnel, a single ladder stood straight up. We both looked to see a metal trap door above. We looked at each other, and Nook knew I didn't want to go first. 'You keep watch here; make sure no one sneaks up behind us.' He told me and took the first rung on the ladder. I nodded, relieved. He made quick work of the ladder, and with a huff, he pushed through the door above, and sunlight streamed down into the tunnel. I could feel his smile as he clambered up and out. His face reappearing, looking down at me delighted. He reached his hand down to beckon me up. I couldn't move; my feet felt like they were glued to the ground. 'Aveline, what's wrong?'

I looked back down the pitch-black tunnel. My chest felt tight, my legs heavy. 'I'm scared.' My voice was small as I looked back up at him. It dawned on him then; this was the furthest I'd ever been from home. I gulped at the thought.

'It's going to be okay. You're going to love it up here.' He stretched down further as if he could reach me and pull me up. I took a deep breath and stepped onto the first rung of the ladder. My heartbeat, faster as I took the next and the next. I swallowed, my hands starting to shake around the metal; I could feel myself losing my grip. I was going to fall. I couldn't keep going. Then I felt Nook's hand on mine. I was closer to the top than I'd realised. I looked up, his face surrounded by the beaming sun; I took his hand and climbed the last few steps.

Location: Salt Glass Lake, The Sovereign City Border

I clambered out onto the soft, plush, green grass that I'd only ever heard about. The breeze was warm here. The blades cool between my fingers. The smell of earth filled my nose. I could hear the sweet song of birds. Smell the salt of the ocean. Everything was so intense, heightened by the fact I'd never experienced them before. I took in a deep breath of fresh, flower-scented air. I looked around to see bright green leafy trees, not a speck of snow in sight. The smell of salt originated from a small lake nestled amongst them. Nook half lifted me to my feet beside him. Almost laughing at me. 'I told you, you'd like it up here.'

'It's so beautiful.' I breathed. 'So, warm.' I smiled, shedding my long coat, and soaked up the sun. Nook did the same. As I took in my new surroundings, Nook retrieved a light blue petalled flower from the flower bed and placed it amongst the braids in my hair.

'Now, you'll never forget this moment.' He smiled.

'I don't think I could ever forget this.' I beamed. 'I've never been so close to the Palace before!' I exclaimed, looking up. The Sovereign City wall was no more than a clear mile from here. I could practically see the perfectly placed white stones it was built from.

'Wait until you see how we get to Salt Glass City.' He grinned at me. Then, he took my hand and guided me towards the lake.

As we got closer, I could see a small platform by the side of the lake. There was a console attached. Nook went up and tapped on the glass screen. '*Select Destination*' An automated voice came out of the console. Nook scrolled through the list of destinations. I watched over his shoulder, reading all the places, some of which I'd never even heard of. *Central Station, Dragon Isle, Light Creek Cove...* the list went on until '*You have selected: Salt Glass City.*' The voice said, '*T-Pod expected arrival, T-minus sixty seconds*.' Nook shuffled us back and held up a hand as if to say, just wait. After a moment, I felt slight vibrations under my feet. I looked through the trees to the small path leading

up to the platform. First, there was nothing. Then the

vibrations became stronger. Suddenly behind us, a large

sphere emerged with force from the Lake, making us

both jump; I turned to Nook,

'I really thought it would come from the other way.'

He shrugged, trying not to laugh. The large Sphere

rolled out of the lake and up onto the platform in front of

us. It was at least six feet tall, maybe more and just as

wide. It was opaque white all the way around. It made a

click sound as it settled in the middle of the platform.

After a moment, it started to spin around slowly until an

outline of a door appeared in front of us. It clicked open,

sliding around the dome shape. I felt my mouth fall open

in awe, watching it. Nook took my hand and pulled me

through. Inside were two rows of three seats opposite

each other, with a table between them. We sat beside each other on the far side. The door slid closed behind us, and after a moment, the sphere jerked forwards and started to roll. 'This is insane!' I grabbed Nook's arm as the ball moved around us. It was like we were floating inside. I felt the pressure as it hit the water and sunk down.

'Wait until you see this.' He said and tapped the table. A screen lit up in front of him, and he clicked a button that read, *View: Open/Closed.* I watched in wonder as the outer of the sphere slid back, revealing nothing more than a clear cover between us and the entire ocean. 'Careful, flies will get in.' Nook said, putting his hand under my chin to close my mouth. I beamed with joy. The ball continued to roll smoothly through the ocean. All around us, sea life swam as if we belonged there.

'How many times have you done this?' I asked curiously; he wasn't anywhere near as excited as I was.

'Only a few, I came with the Chief a few times on official business.' He put both our chairs back and relaxed into his seat, watching the colours of the sea above us. I did the same.

'Are you excited about becoming the Chief one day?' I asked, pointing at a bright pink fish as it swam right up close to us.

'I guess. I'll be the first boy Chief in like, five generations, though.'

What if I mess up? I thought the rest of his sentence. 'You won't.' I smiled. 'I'll make sure of it.'

'We need to make sure we *can* go back first.' He sat up again; I mirrored him. 'We need to find out who you are.'

'Find out who's after me, you mean?'

'The King must've known. He must've been protecting you somehow.'

'Someone found out and killed him so he couldn't warn me… Why would the King know who I was, though?' I queried, my head in my hand. 'Chief Eire knew more, something she didn't want to tell us.'

'Do you think she got something in return for keeping you locked away in the Pink Mountains?' He asked the question I couldn't bring myself to.

I bit my lip in reply, realising what an evil thought that was. Chief Eire wasn't evil. She loved me. As much as anyone could love a child, that wasn't theirs to love.

'Nook?'

'Yeah?'

'Do you think my real parents are still alive?' I could feel the hope creeping into my heart and the fear running through my veins. *Did I want them to be alive?*

'Of course, you'd want to meet them if they were.' He put a hand on my shoulder. A second of surprise, that he knew what I was thinking. 'But I don't know. If they were, why weren't they keeping you safe instead of the Chief?'

'And what does the King have to do with it?' I sighed, sinking back into my chair.

'Someone must know who you are. We just need to find someone who was around when we were born.'

'Someone that we trust.' I corrected him.

'The Salt Glass Queen might know; Mum said she's always learning what she can about the other lands so she can use it against them.' He rolled his eyes.

'Do you think she knew about me then?'

'I don't think so. No one's ever seen you. No one outside of the Pink Mountains even knows you exist.'

'Except King Petri.' I corrected him. *Who knows who else…?*

'At least we know they're on your side. If they've known all this time, they've been keeping it a secret.' Nook argued.

'Until they didn't.' I replied. We both exhaled, realising *someone gave me up.*

Nook nodded in agreement. I dropped my head back into the chair and closed my eyes, the beauty of the ocean no longer subduing my growing fear. 'What if he knew I was dangerous?' I said softly. 'What if King Petri sent me far enough away that I couldn't damage The Sovereign City?'

'You're not dangerous.' Nook said adamantly. 'You can't even block a punch.' He laughed, flicking my still bruised nose.

'Ow!' I batted his hand away, and we both laughed. 'Woe…' I sat up, staring out the clear glass into the ocean. 'What is that?' I asked, mouth open, as I stared at the thinly furred creature swimming around us. It was the colour of the ocean, barely visible, a fine, pointed fin on its back, webbed feet. I looked closer to see it had shiny blue scales intermixed with its fur that moved and shifted with it.

'That's a havsvarg.' Nook's eyes went wide. 'I've only seen one once before. Never this close, though.' We both reached up to touch the glass as if we could feel it.

'It's so fast.' I watched it swim circles around us. Then, as I looked back to Nook, I was taken by an even more wondrous sight. 'Is that… Salt Glass City?' I asked, staring at the beautiful glass structure sitting at the bottom of the ocean behind him. It was lit up, sparkling almost in the dark of the water. It looked so delicate yet held up towers and archways. It was a hub of activity as all around it, the people of Salt Glass City swam in and out, mingled by doorways and interacted with the local sea life. Their scaled tails, elegant in the water, shimmering like the glass of the city.

'That's it.' He replied, turning to look at it. The T-Pod smoothly rolled towards the west side of the city.

The havsvarg swam off as we got closer. A part of the

wall started to separate, a hole the perfect size for the T-

Pod to enter.

Location: Salt Glass City, Station

The T-Pod rolled into the large domed room made of

glass. Slowly we sank to the floor, and as we touched

down, the seawater drained out of the room. A moment

later, the T-Pod closed into its opaque covering, and the

door slid open. Cautiously, I exited first to Nook'

surprise. I couldn't wait to see the city up close. I thought the floor would be cold, but as I reached down and brushed it with my fingertips, there was a warmth that radiated from the glass. It shimmered a pink-gold colour. I looked around in awe as Nook started towards a set of double doors across the room. I hurried after him, almost slipping. My boots had no traction on the smooth glass. I grabbed onto Nook as I almost flew out the doors when I caught up to him.

The hallway was empty. On the west wall was sheer glass that looked out onto the ocean. I peered through; we were three floors up, and below was a courtyard. 'Don't get too close.' Nook pulled me away 'We don't want to attract attention.' He said as we walked to the other side of the hallway.

'What *are* we looking for?' I asked as we approached a lobby area. There were five lifts, a small seating area and a large, curved desk but not a soul in sight. 'And where is everybody?'

'This is the safest hour to swim freely in the oceans. The temperature drops, and the larger creatures retreat outwards into the warmth.'

'The havsvarg wasn't a large creature?' I looked at him, shocked.

'A baby compared to what else is out there.' He stopped in the middle of the lobby and looked around, a large sigh. 'Can't you have another vision or something? You brought us here.' He put his hands on his hips, looking for a sign.

'I can't control it.' I replied, looking around desperately for something that could point us in the right direction. A prominent rectangular water feature on the wall above the lobby suddenly came alive with a projected image. It was a news alert. We both looked. A woman from The Sovereign City was on the screen, followed by a video of Nook and I escaping camp into the woods. They enlarged the image to show our faces. Both our faces dropped as we watched the projected water-screen.

'Lord Ellis is enforcing a shutdown until these two prime suspects are found. They're believed to be responsible for King Petri's murder.'

'He can't do this!' Nook exclaimed.

'All transport will be halted between the lands Trade will stop. All communication will be blocked until the investigation into King Petri's murder has been closed.' The woman continued to announce. 'Anyone seen to be aiding the two perpetrators will risk

imprisonment on Dragon Isle. They are considered

extremely dangerous. Do not attempt to make contact.'

She finished with a grave tone. We both watched,

speechless. They continued to play the video of us

running away from the CSC soldiers at the camp.

'This is bad. This is so bad. This has been broadcast

all over Azzurra.' Nook began to ramble.

'Umm… Nook?' I tapped at his shoulder as a tall,

muscular man appeared from one of the lifts. His clothes

were embedded into him like the scales of the

havsvarg's were to its fur. Moved with him. Shimmered

as he walked. The man headed towards us; it was as if he

were in a trance the way he stared at me.

'Prince Nuri.' Nook tilted his head in respect as the

man approached.

'Son of Eire.' Nuri bowed in response. His eyes still on me, I copied Nook's action, but Nuri was looking at me as though he'd seen a ghost. He was lost for words, staring at me as if I'd hurt him in some way.

'Prince Nuri?' Nook looked between us, confused. Nuri stammered a few times before managing to get his sentence out.

'Forgive me I… You look just like- 'he shook the thought away before finishing it. Nook and I shared another look; *Nuri knows something.* We were agreed.

'I look like who?' I asked softly. Nuri continued to stare at me in disbelief.

'Someone I used to know.' A smile crept across his face; a memory warmed his heart. He extended his hand to me; I saw it had a faint pink-gold, liquid circle. *A permanent Scion?* I thought, and Nook nodded as if in answer. I shook Nuri's hand with my black taped one. As I did, I got that warm feeling shoot through me again. I held his hand tight, desperately clung to it as I struggled to catch my breath again.

'Aveline!' Nook exclaimed, grabbing my shoulder, trying to keep me from fading out.

'Aveline?' Nuri's face dropped in horror, but it was starting to fade along with Nook and the rest of the room. Replaced by another room in Salt Glass City. Tall, open, large translucent windows, looking out into the ocean. Velvet cushioned sofas. I felt Nuri hug me close, wrap his giant arms around me as I continued to grip his hand with all my might. A door opened in the large room; feet shuffled in. Then I saw her again, the older me, but this time Nuri was there. Younger. A teenager, too. He pulled me onto the sofa next to him; we were both laughing.

'So, what do you say, dinner and a show in The Sovereign City?' The younger Nuri asked me, pushing a fallen piece of hair from my face.

'I can't, tonight. I'm seeing-'

'Yes, the *soldier*. How could I forget.' He sounded annoyed, sat forward away from me. I sat forward too, placed my hand around his arm, my head on his shoulder.

'Don't be that way. Another night-'

'You won't keep him a secret forever. Your father *will* find out if he doesn't know already ' Nuri placed his hand over mine, a small smile, but he had sadness in his eyes.

'You'd be surprised what I can keep secret.' I reached up and kissed his cheek, grinned back at him. I could feel Nuri holding me tighter, hear Nook saying my name. Then, the room started to fade away; as it did, the older me caught my eye again, and it was almost as if she mouthed the words, *Aveline…*

'Aveline.' Nuri stroked down my hair as I loosened my grip on his hand. My focus returned; I blinked away the vision and slowly pushed away from him without argument. Nook grabbed me, held me as I stared at Nuri, confused. He looked at the black tape on my hand. He didn't need to see my skin to know what would be there.

'You know who I am.' I told, not asked him. He stared back at me, afraid.

He nodded, slowly. 'You're supposed to be dead….' The words fell from Nuri's mouth.

Nook and I stared back, horrified.

Location: Salt Glass City, Station

Nuri shuffled us both through the double doors we'd left through only minutes earlier. He was on edge, distracted, checking no one was following us. He shut and locked the doors behind us. 'Prince Nuri.' I demanded.

'You can't be here. It's not safe.' He replied and walked over to the sphere platform. 'I'll order you a T-Pod to take you back to the Pink Mountains.'

'We can't go back.' Nook told him as we hurried to catch up to him. 'They came for her there, already. That's why we left.'

'We can't go anywhere. You saw that news alert.' I crossed my arms over my chest. Nuri looked at me, hurt again. 'We need to figure this out. Fight back. What do you know? What do you mean I'm supposed to be dead?'

I'm sorry we don't have time. Queen Cabeira will be back soon, and if she sees you if she finds out you were here... you will never be safe.'

'Why does she want to hurt Aveline?' Nook asked for both of us.

'She doesn't want to hurt you, but if she finds out you're alive, she'll think your mother is too.'

'Is she?' My voice did that cracking thing again that I didn't consent to. Nuri stared at me for a moment, almost as though he could love me.

'Looking at you, I don't know anymore.' He replied softly. 'Please let me protect you. Leave here.'

I nodded in reply.

'Where do we go?' Nook asked.

Nuri thought for a moment. Then an idea came to him. 'Light Creek Cove. I'll meet you there later when I can get away without drawing suspicion.' Nuri told us; I recognised the name from the console list and looked to Nook.

'It's in the unclaimed.' He told me, answering without me having to ask.

'Which means you should be safe from anyone wanting to hurt you or use you.' He tapped on the console to set the destination for the T-Pod still sitting there from our arrival. When he was done, he turned to me, knelt to my level. 'You have to be careful, Aveline. Don't tell anyone your name or where you've been. He'll hurt anyone to get to you.'

'Who will?' I breathed back.

'Lord Ellis. He's the reason you were killed. Why your mother was too.' I could swear I saw tears starting to form in the backs of his eyes as he spoke.

'But I'm alive….'

'And I hope, somewhere your mother is too, but I have no doubt she would've done anything to keep you safe. Including sacrificing herself.' He stroked the side of my face; I realised now that he was seeing her when he looked at me.

'It's her I keep seeing, isn't it?' I whispered. 'In my visions, it's not the future. It's the past. Her past.' I pursed my lips, not sure how I felt at that moment. Happy I'd seen my mother for the first time in my entire life. Sad that I may never truly see her in person. Guilty, that I had been the reason she was dead and afraid that *I may not live long enough to know the truth.* At that moment, Nook took my hand. He was inside my head again. A serious look on his face and his other hand around the hilt of his dagger at his waist, *I won't let anyone hurt you.* I believed him.

'You have to go now.' Nuri hurried us into the open T-Pod. He reached in, wrapped his arms around me and held me in the warmest embrace for just a moment.

Then, with his hand still on the back of my neck, he held me there and looked me in the eye as he spoke. 'There are people throughout the lands that will protect you. People still loyal to your mother.' He looked to Nook, 'just be careful, trust yourself. Your mum had the best instincts of anyone I've ever known.' He finished with a single nod and pushed me lightly back into the T-Pod.

'Wait, what about Azzurra? Lord Ellis? We can't just let him do this.' I argued back.

'This is not your fight Aveline.' Nuri replied sternly. 'You need to hide and stay hidden until this is over.' He pushed me back into the T-Pod and shut the door.

Location: The Unclaimed, Light Creek Cove

The T-Pod rolled along the cliffs, so close I thought one

strong wind would blow us straight over into the sea.

The landscape was like nothing I'd ever seen before. So

bright, colourful, everything looked so alive. We jolted

to a sudden stop halfway down the hill. 'What

happened?' I asked, looking out to see we were

suspended.

'I don't know.' Nook replied and tapped on the console table. A message came up, T-Pod service, DISABLED. 'It's Lord Ellis. He stopped all transport.' He said as the door clicked open. We both looked.

'How much further is it?' I asked, looking out into the sea of green grass and sharp-edged rocks of the hill face and nothing else.

'Does it matter?' He looked back. We had no other choice. We both sighed and clambered out of the T-Pod. Nook dropped gracefully down onto the grass while I flailed and kicked to hit the ground below me. Nook steadied me, and we started by foot up the hill. It was more like a climb as we got to the top. The rocks, hard on our skin as we hauled ourselves higher. My foot slipped a few times. Our boots, not built for the terrain. The grass gave way under Nook's hand, and he fell, his face grazing down the jagged rocks. His blood drops hit my forehead.

'Are you okay?' I called up. I watched him touch the fresh wound on his cheek. He nodded.

'Just keep moving. We're almost there.' He grunted as he pulled himself the last of the way up. I felt his hand on mine, helping me over the final hurdle. As he pulled me up, my weight toppled us over, and we rolled down over the hill the other side. The jagged rocks, now soft green grass. We rolled to a stop at the bottom of the hill, and I felt the grass turn to sand. I looked down to see a light coating of pink sand all over me. The sand stretched as far as I could see. Disappearing under the sea and enclosed in a hilly alcove. It was suddenly ten degrees warmer, the sun a little brighter, and there was music in the air. Acoustic, echoing up from below. I looked around to see a lighthouse, beige with a white door, sat upon the small hill where we stood. Below us, an entire village on water, connected by flat bridges. It was incredible. Only a metre or so above water but a place entirely of its own. Nook appeared next to me; he looked just as amazed.

'You've never been here before?' I commented.

'I've only heard stories. We never had reason to come here.' He replied, in awe of the scene in front of us.

'No wonder everyone was fighting for it.' I dropped to my knees. Let the fine pink sand bury my hands. It was so soft, silky almost. It covered the land as far as the water's edge. The water wasn't the deep blue of the ocean Salt Glass City was in, but green, clear water. I could see through it all the way to the bottom. Behind us on the rocks, a creature bounded up. Small, furry with big, pointed ears. Two fluffy tails that ended in a black tip against the rest of its grey fur. I turned in time to see it hop down and stalk towards us. As its paws hit the sand, its grey fur turned to match the pink of the sand. I had to do a double take to be sure what I'd seen. The black tips of its tail trailed the ground behind it, leaving a mark in the sand. I tapped Nook hurriedly to get his attention. He turned to see where I was pointing but couldn't see it at first. It was less than a metre from us now. I held my hands up as if to say stop, and it froze in place. Sat up, flicked its tail around and revealed its position to Nook.

'Woe.' The noise fell from Nook's mouth. The creature continued to stare at me. It sniffed the air between us. 'It's a poison-tipped mimic.'

'A what?' I asked, too afraid to look away from it. It got to its feet again and sauntered towards us. Its eyes, big, golden, innocent. Slowly, I knelt, my palms open, extended. Nook looked at me as if I were crazy. Then, cautiously, the creature came closer. Sniffed my fingertips, and then, it did the strangest thing of all; it seemed to bow.

'Is it doing what I think it's doing?' Nook asked, amazed.

'I think so…' I replied just as bemused. I reached out and scratched the creature behind the ears; it seemed to like it. It rubbed its head in my hand; it was so soft. Its fur changed to match the black of the tape around my hand. 'I'm going to call you Goldie.' I said, looking into its sparkling eyes.

'I don't think acquiring pets is on the to-do list.'
Nook crossed his arms, unimpressed.

'Everyone deserves a name that doesn't make them
sound like a threat.' I retorted. Nook rolled his eyes.

'It has that name for a reason. Its tail is so
poisonous, one prick, and you'll be dead by your next
breath.'

'Then I suppose we should be nice to it.' I said,
straightening up. I looked around, up at the lighthouse. It
had a large arched doorway. Nook followed my gaze.
We were both starting to feel the heat of the sun. Our
warm boots and thermals, making us overheat. 'I think
it's safer than going into the village.' I suggested. Nook
nodded and took the first steps towards it. Goldie
followed us, intrigued. Its tiny paws, silent on the sand.
If it weren't for its large ears, it wouldn't even be as tall

as my knee from the ground. Nook knocked on the door. Nothing. He tried the round handle. It was unlocked. He let the door fall open into the room. A single candle was lit on the round table inside. We both peered in. Goldie crept through our legs to look in as well. Nook and I shared a look of curiosity and trepidation. ZOOM! Something flew through the sky above us. Nook grabbed my arm and shoved me through the doorway. He left just a crack for us to see through and for Goldie to slip inside.

'What, what's going on?' I shout whispered.

'That was a Cloud Ship Command SkySearcher.' Nook whispered back. 'The CSC shouldn't be flying over here. The airspace is part of the land too.'

'You think they're looking for us?' I gulped; as I did, Goldie poised for attack, tails up, pointed forward, ready to pounce.

'I don't think we're in any place to be relying on coincidence.' Nook's brow furrowed back at me. I leant down and stroked Goldie's ears to calm the creature as we peered back out through the crack to see a one-man flight ship skimming over the village. I closed the door and held it shut.

'Well, I guess we better make ourselves comfortable for now.' I turned and leant back on the door.

'Do you think Nuri set us up?' Nook stepped back and looked at me seriously.

'No, I don't think so.'

'How can you not even consider the possibility? He's the one who sent us here.'

'He loved my mother with all his heart. I felt it. He would never hurt me. Not if it meant hurting her.'

'Then we could've been followed. Or someone else saw us. We need to be more careful.' Nook was suddenly focused; it reminded me of how he was in training. Confident and alert. A leader. 'Okay, we stay here until the SkySearcher has passed. We give Nuri until dusk. Then we move again.'

I nodded in agreement, despite knowing we had nowhere to go, and stepped away from the door. The floorboards creaked underfoot. Looking around, I saw a coat rack on one wall with a single coat and a pair of boots. Nook followed my gaze.

'Maybe they didn't hear us?' He suggested. There was a curved staircase following the lighthouse upwards. Slowly, we ascended.

Location: Light Creek Cove, Lighthouse

The staircase opened into a large open room. There was
a kitchen space, living room and eating area. It was dark,
the windows were small, and let in only a fraction of
light. It looked lived in. Blankets and cushions, scattered
across the sofa. A cup of tea, half-drunk, on the built-in
seat by the window. I got a shiver down my spine,

looking around. Nook crossed the threshold of the room first. Walked over to the wooden table that was scattered with papers and pens. 'Hey, come look at this.' He called out. I walked over, arms hugging myself, to see a map of Azzurra laid out on the table. Pinned down in each corner.

'I never knew it was so big.' I scanned across the markings, all the lands and the territories outlined. Goldie hopped up onto the table beside us. I stroked down its back, calmingly.

'Look, all the smuggler tunnels are marked.' Nook pointed to the dotted lines that ran throughout the map. 'This one goes all the way to The Sovereign City Palace.' He traced the line from the Arid land. 'This could be how The King's assailant got to him.'

'That's in Chief Keahi's boundary.' I pointed out. We shared a concerned look. 'He wouldn't... would he?'

'No. Never. He'd never betray us.'

'Never?' I said softly. Nook looked back at me, less convinced. I looked closer at the map. In the corner was a signet. I ran my finger over it. A sharp breath caught my lungs, and it was happening again, but this time it lasted only a second. Just long enough for me to see the map hanging on a wall and a woman's hands, taking it down. I let out my breath as my eyes refocused.

'What did you see?' Nook grabbed my hand.

'I think someone stole this map.' I breathed heavy, 'It was so fast.'

'That's the signet for the Sovereigns of the City; it would've been kept in the Palace.' Nook thought out loud. 'Every land has one; ours is rolled up in the Chief's

Chambers, in that leather-bound cylinder.' He continued as he slowly unpinned the top left corner of the map.

'What are you doing?'

'Seeing, who it belongs to.' He replied as he unpinned the bottom left corner and pulled it back delicately. On the back, in ink, a list of names of all the rulers of The Sovereign City. The first two names were inscribed as *Queen Nara and King Han*. We read down the list of only four name pairings until we got to the last two: *King Petri and Queen Cicera*. 'That's the late King. This was stolen since he was crowned forty years ago.'

'Who, would steal his map if every land has one?' I frowned, trying to piece together a plausible explanation.

'Well, every ruled land.' Nook corrected. He pointed to the Unclaimed land on the map, to drawings of ships on the far West Ocean labelled Moon Whisperer's, then to the Blue Forrest in the Northwest above the Arid land, and the city in the clouds, the CSC. 'None of these places would have one.'

'So, someone that doesn't belong in their land anymore stole the map….' I thought out loud.

'That describes us now too, you know.' Nook pinned the map back down.

'A map *would* be helpful….' I smirked. Nook shoved me lightly in disbelief. 'Do you think whoever's living here will come back?' I looked around for clues as to who it could be.

'I don't think they've been here in a while.' Nook replied, stepping further into the room. He walked to the fridge and opened it. Empty but for two tubs of Squigglepop. He took them both out and handed one to me.

'Nook, we can't.'

'No one's been here in weeks. Maybe months.' He shook the tub at me to take it. 'I spend all day learning how to track; trust me, the trail here is cold.'

I relented and took the tub of Squigglepop, suddenly starving; Nook fetched two forks from a drawer and handed me one. We sat on the sofa and demolished both tubs. 'This stuff is SO good; why do we never have it at home?' I asked, shovelling another mouthful down me.

'It's hard to get; a lot of it gets sent to the CSC because it lasts so long.' Nook replied with his mouth still full. 'They have a deal with the City Sovereign's.'

'What do they get in return?'

'Their soldiers if they ever need them.'

'Like if we go to war?' I set the rest of my tub on the table. My words made Nook freeze.

'Yeah, like if we go to war…' he set his tub down too. ZOOM! The SkySearcher, whizzed past the lighthouse at rocket speed. We both snapped our heads to look. 'I think it's leaving.' He crept to the small window by the built-in seat and peered through the glass. 'Yeah, it's gone; I can see its smoke trail in the distance.' He continued as he sat back. I walked over and perched next to him. I leant into him, our heads together, our sighs in unison.

'What do you think he will do to Azzurra?' I whispered.

'Nothing good.' Nook replied, disheartened. 'Nothing worse than what he will do to you.' He lifted his head and met my eye. 'We have to find a safe place for you. Where he can't find you.'

'No. I can't hide forever. We need to find a way to save Azzurra.'

'Aveline. We can't save the entire world. The rulers will figure out how to dethrone Lord Ellis. We just need to keep you out of his hands.' Nook got to his feet adamantly.

'We can't sit and do nothing. He's shutting The Sovereign City off from everyone.'

'He's cornering you. Forcing you out.' Nook was getting angry. We never fought. 'He's trying to isolate you, so there's no one to protect you.' He grabbed me by the shoulders, his eyes darting between mine. He wasn't angry.

'I'm scared too, Nook.' I wrapped my arms around him and held him tight. He hugged me back. I pulled away and saw the deep scratch still on his face; I wiped some of the blood away. 'Maybe they have a first aid kit around here.' I smiled.

I stood in the small bedroom. It opened out off a small, curved hallway behind the kitchen; no door separated the two rooms. There was a small bathroom through an open archway, off the bedroom. I stood in front of the beige wall between the two rooms. Nook's footsteps echoed towards me. I didn't look; I couldn't. I was stopped in my tracks by a chalk drawing on the blank wall in front of me. It was a mix of purple and orange, and it was an exact copy of the wooden, arched door with the flower painted on it from my vision.

'Did you find anything? You've been ages?' Nook's voice broke into the room. I didn't reply. I continued to stare with the illustrator firmly in my hand. Nook walked to stand next to me. 'What did you do?' He looked from the drawing to the illustrator.

'Nothing.' I replied. 'It was already here….'

'Is that the same door-'

'From my first vision? Yep.' I interrupted. We both stared at the drawing of the door. 'Do you know what this is?' I held the illustrator between us. He shook his head. 'The Chief, the elder's, your mum *never* mentioned anything? *Ever?*'

'Not once. I know as much as you do about Scions.' He replied.

'I only know what we learnt in class. You knew Nuri's was permanent.' I tucked the illustrator back into my boot.

'Yeah, but that's all I know. Some Scion Aura's don't go away. Nuri's makes him adept at surviving in the water. It allows him to switch between his sea and his human form.' Nook explained a little defensively. 'I only know that because I asked the Chief the first time, she took me to Salt Glass City.' *I swear.* His face said the rest.

I'm sorry. Mine replied.

'Do you think your mum drew this?' Nook gestured back to the drawing. 'Did you touch it?' I knew what he meant. *Did I get another vision?*

'Yeah. I didn't see anything….' I said as I tried again. Traced the lines. The handle. Nothing.

'Then maybe it's not important?' Nook shrugged. I wasn't convinced.

'I thought we weren't in a place where we could rely on coincidence?' I cocked a brow. Nook took a deep breath, let out an almighty sigh. Something out the window drew his eye. I looked too. A shadow fell over us. We both went to the window to see the sky turn black. Darkness swept over Azzurra. The clouds, menacing. Alive. With flecks of deep blue. 'That doesn't look good. Has there been another murder?'

'That's not a mourning signal.' Nook looked concerned. As concerned as Chief Eire had looked.

Part Three

Hope Is what pulls you from the darkest of places; Love is what keeps you from falling back

Location: Lighthouse, Light Creek Cove

We rushed to the front door and stepped out into an icy breeze as the clouds became thicker, darker, swirled around above us. The pink sands looked grey under the shadow, the flowers wilted, and the music that had been scoring our time here ceased abruptly. 'What's going on?'

I half-shouted over the strong wind. Goldie hid between my legs, the creature's fur fluttering around it. Goldie dug its claws deep into my boot to keep from flying away.

'I think we're at war!' Nook shouted back. 'That's Blue Magic.' He pointed to the blue flecks swirling amongst the clouds. 'Someone's released the Blue Forrest. They're trying to take power over Azzurra!' He grabbed my hand, held it tight as we tried to block our eyes from the growing wind with our other.

'What do we do?!' I yelled back; not sure my voice hadn't been swept away in the growing storm. Then, as we looked around for a sign of hope, six SkySearchers appeared in the black clouds. Their lights zeroed in on us like spotlights from the sky.

'RUN!' Nook yelled. We sprinted away from the lighthouse and down towards the village. The spotlights following us as we slipped and trudged through the sand as fast as we could. Goldie bounding along beside us, dodging the beams of light. The SkySearchers got closer and closer. They started firing bolts of electric currents. I screamed as one hit the sand, just a metre in front of me. The sand shot up into the air around me on impact. I fell back as another one hit just to the side of me. 'Aveline!' I heard Nook call out for me. WHOOSH! WHOOSH! WHOOSH! Shot after shot came at the sand around me. I couldn't run; I couldn't get away. I didn't even know which way was forward anymore as the sand created a falling wall around me. The next thing I knew, Nook was flying towards me. He launched himself through the wall of sand and knocked me back. He landed in a roll while I landed in a heap on the other side of the sand.

WHOOSH! Another shot, this one so close I felt the heat

come off the electric bolt. Goldie pounced on it in front

of me. I looked up to see another coming straight for me.

I couldn't watch. I ducked, covering my face with my

arms at the same time Nook reached for me. That

sensation hit again.

My footprints and a cloud of blue smoke were all

that was left in the sand when Nook grabbed for thin air.

Location: Dark Forrest, The Sovereign City Boundary

I landed in a tumble on the cold ground. It was covered in leaves and dried mud. I looked around to find myself alone, lost, in the dark, creepy woods. The shadows moved around me. The trees towering around me. Closing me in. I couldn't even see the black of the sky through the dense foliage of the leaves. 'Nook?' I called out. My voice small, timid. *Nothing*. I shivered, my thermals and boots suddenly not enough. I sat, hugging my legs, feeling a sudden wave of exhaustion hit.

Behind me, a rustle in the bushes. My eyes shot wide,

the adrenaline fighting the fatigue. My heart beat a little

faster, my breathing slowed as I felt the creature prowl

out behind me. I couldn't move. I was frozen. I could

hear its low growl as it began to circle me. I could see it

then, out of the corner of my eye. My lip trembled as its

eye met mine. It was the size of the snow beast. Black.

No, deep green and Lean. Muscular. It bared its pointed

teeth at me. Its eyes were hypnotic. It snarled at me,

making me flinch as it continued to stare me down. I

hugged myself tighter as it crept around in front of me. It

skulked closer. I could feel the heat of its breath on my

face. It curled its lips back, opened its jaw. I didn't dare

look away; I held its eye with all the courage I had. It

was about to bite down when suddenly the beast

pounced. I watched; eyes wide as it flew straight over my head. So, close I felt its belly fur on my hair. I flicked my head around to see the beasty pinning down a woman. Beside her, a man in a uniform I'd never seen before. He looked important. He fired two shots straight up into the air. It was the same kind of gun the SkySearchers had. *He was CSC.* I sucked in a breath as I forced myself to my feet. The beasty spooked by the shots, leapt off the woman, snarled at them, tail pointed. The woman pulled out a sword from the sheath at her waist and dared the beasty.

'No!' The man shouted. 'Don't hurt it.' He told her.

'It wouldn't take mercy on us.' She spat back. I could see blood dripping down her arm from the beasty's claws. The beasty moved between us. Snarling. The fatigue was winning over. I could feel my legs giving way beneath me. My eyelids, fighting to stay open.

'It's worth more alive than you are.' The man grabbed her arm, willed her to lower her sword.

'It's deadly,' She reluctantly lowered her blade, sheathed it again.

'Only if you look it in the eye.' The man corrected her as I fell to my knees. The beasty moved close to me. I could feel the warmth of its body heat radiating towards me, but I didn't feel afraid anymore. I felt safe in its presence. BANG! BANG! The man shot into the air again, frightening the beasty. He leapt back and forth before darting into the shrubbery again. I could feel its eyes on me, peeking out through the leaves as I fell the rest of the way to the floor. The ground cool on my cheek. The earth, fresh in my nose. I felt hands on me. Turning me over. The woman's face over mine.

'What's wrong with her?' The man asked. My eyelids fluttering closed; he was just a haze now.

'The travel has exhausted her. She's not used to her power.' The woman cupped the base of my neck. My eyes drifted open again. I could make out the curls of her hair, her soft eyes.

'Help me…' I heard my voice as if it wasn't a part of me.

'Don't worry, little spark, we're taking you exactly where you need to be.' The woman smiled as she pulled me into her arms. I felt myself lift into the air; my head fall back. Their footsteps faded away as my mind went blank.

Location: The City Palace, The King's office

I woke to their voices. My eyes, not ready to open; I wasn't sure if I was dreaming or not, at first.

'We were a mile away!' It was the same voice as the woman from the forest. She was angry.

'I'm sorry, she's hard to pin down.' A smaller, sweeter voice replied.

'You had one job. Find the girl.' The woman's angry voice came again. I forced my eyes to open. I saw her, she was hazy, but I was sure when same curls came into view. She was talking to a younger woman, a teenager.

'I *did*, but it's like she's in two places at once sometimes. I don't see her as clearly as others.' The girl was upset, afraid of the woman. They both turned to look at me then. I struggled to sit up. My body, weak, my arms buckling under my own weight. The sofa, a plump velvet beneath me. I skimmed the room as my focus came back. It was regal, expensive, sofas, a desk, large windows with heavy curtains on either side.

'Where am I?' I asked, rubbing my eyes awake. The younger girl came towards me. She was in platform shoes, making her seem taller than she was and a flowery top. The colours caught my eye, everything else in the room being so dark.

'You're at The Sovereign Palace.' She told me. Her hand gently on my knee. 'I'm Zosime.' She smiled, so sweetly, so lovingly. She reached over, wiped the dried earth from my cheek. I looked to the curly-haired woman, standing, staring at me, from across the room. 'That's Selene.' Zosime said. I could see her clearly now; she didn't look as friendly as I remembered. Her arm was bandaged now. Her sword, still at her side, she had long, thick boots. A tailored coat. A ring on every finger and five different necklaces. She didn't belong to The Sovereigns; I could tell that much. The Moon Whisperer's maybe. I wasn't sure who Zosime belonged to, though.

'It's rude to stare, little spark.' Selene spoke. Her voice was cold. Soulless. A knock came at the door. 'Enter.' Selene called out. The door opened, and the important-looking man from the forest entered. 'Captain Azaevior.' Selene announced.

He didn't even look at me. He walked straight to Selene and whispered something in her ear; she kept her eye on me the entire time. Then he left again without so much as a glance in my direction. 'Keep an eye on her.' Selene ordered Zosime. 'He'll be here soon.' Selene smiled at me then. Not a warm smile that brought hope but a menacing one that told me I wasn't going to like what happened next.

Selene left promptly after Captain Azaevior. Zosime cleaned the dirt from my skin, removed my braids and brushed out the knots. 'Are you hurt?' She asked as she twirled the ends of my hair into ringlets. I shook my head. 'You've been asleep a long while.' She told me; her hand traced from the ends of my hair down to my palm. She started to unwrap the tape, I pulled back.

Aveline.

The words pushed through my brain. I tried to hide my surprise so Zosime wouldn't notice.

Aveline, are you there? It was Nook's voice. The words were muffled, but I was sure it was him.

'Could I get some water?' I asked Zosime, forcing a dry cough.

'Of course. I'll be right back.' She said and left the room.

Nook? I thought as hard as I could. I walked over to the tall floor-length windows behind the desk and looked out. The room looked over the Palace Gardens. I imagined they were once perfectly kept, with flowers of every colour and somewhere you would walk on a sunny day. Now they were wilted and dark and dripping with sorrow. *Nook, can you hear me?* I pushed the thought harder. Willed it out the window and across the land as far as it would go. Disappointment filled my face. The sky was even darker somehow. Dragons now swarmed the sky. Their fiery breath piercing through the clouds. The door opened behind me. Zosime, a glass of water in hand,

'What are you doing?' She asked, placing the water down on the side table.

'There are dragons.' I replied. 'What's happening to Azzurra?'

'It's dying.' She spoke softly as she walked towards me. 'But *You* can save it. Save all of us.' She continued as I backed into the window. My hand, on the latch, to open it.

'Why me?' I gripped the handle tight.

'You're special, Aveline. You're what we've been waiting for.' She smiled. Her hand brushed down my now curly hair. 'You have the power to change everything.' She took my taped hand again. 'You don't have to hide anymore.' She unpinned the tape, let it fall away. 'You should never have had to hide.' She held my hand, stroked my palm. As she did, the purple circle presented itself; she opened her palm to show she had the same one.

'You're like me?' I gasped, my hand loosening on the latch.

'There's not a single person in this world like you, Aveline.' She closed her hand, and our circles faded away. The door opened again; this time, it was Selene. Zosime didn't look happy to see her. Selene walked at me determinedly. I stepped back, opening the window as I did. A gust of wind shot into the room. My hair billowed around me. I stood, my heels over the edge, the window two floors up from the ground.

'What are you doing?' Selene spat.

'I won't go with you.' I shouted at her. Zosime stood to the side in shock. The window started to shake in the wind. I wasn't sure how long I could hold on, but I was sure wherever Selene was taking me would be worse.

'As defiant as her mother.' Selene grunted, and I swear I could see the beginnings of a smile on Zosime's face. Selene lunged for me. I screamed as I let go. I fell for only a second before Selene's grip was around my wrist, dangling me over the edge. I fought her as she tried to pull me up, but she was stronger than she looked. She hauled me up through the window, tossed me across the room; I hit the desk hard and fell back. The window slammed shut behind me. I looked up to see her storming towards me; I saw it then, on her palm, a green circle; the Warrior Scion. *No wonder she was so strong.* The next thing I knew, Selene was grabbing my wrist and dragging me out of the room.

She dragged me down the carpeted hallway. 'Let me go!' I shouted, trying to tug my arm back. I could see

Zosime watching from the doorway in horror, but she did nothing to help me. 'Please, let me go!' I shouted again. I looked up to see her hand gripped tight around my skin. Then I noticed my hand, and I was reminded how I'd ended up here. So, I tried, I tried with all my might to make myself disappear. I thought of Nook, closed my eyes tight and willed myself away. I could feel the icy breeze hit my lungs. The frost on my skin. The Palace faded, and I could see Nook. He was trudging through the snow towards camp. Alone. Cold. I could feel his determination. There was Goldie, curled in his arms, wrapped in his coat. His grazed face had been bandaged.

Aveline? I heard his voice. He stopped mid-stride as a hallucination of me appeared in front of him.

Nook!

Aveline! I thought I'd lost you! You've been gone for so long. He said, relieved. I could see him clearly. I was like a projection of his mind, but I could feel what he felt. Like we were connected. The storm was harsh, icy, burning our skin.

I'm at The Sovereign Palace. I was kidnapped. I don't know where they're taking me-

We're coming for you. A rebellion has started; everyone's gearing up for war, Nook's thought stopped abruptly, and he began to scream. In front of him, a giant, winged beast sprinted towards him. Its mane blowing in the wind, its paws, the size of Nook's face, thumping across the snow.

RUN! I yelled my thoughts as hard as I could, but as Nook took off in a run, I felt my airway start to close. Selene had stopped. I was no longer sliding along the carpet. I could see her; she was hazy, masked by the snow, blocking my view of Nook.

'What are you doing?' She demanded; still holding my wrist, she stared at the purple circle on my palm. 'You're an *Oracle*?'

AAAAH!! I could just hear Nook continuing to scream in my head; his heart was beating fast, he was terrified. I was stuck between the two places; I could feel Selene' grip around my neck.

'Stop it. Stop it right now!' Selene shook me. I gasped for air. Nook was slipping away. I couldn't see him anymore, just the snow. The white field I'd once called home was falling out of my grasp too. I grabbed Selene's wrist with both hands, tried to pull myself free. My eyes refocused, and she slapped me hard across the cheek. I fell to the side. The carpet, a welcome landing.

Before I could look up, Selene's grip was around my arm and hauling me to my feet. She was breathing hard. Angry. 'They should've killed you the day you were born.'

'What do you want with me? Why me?' I coughed and spluttered my demand.

She leant down close, her face inches from mine. 'Because Lord Ellis promised me everything if I helped him take over.' She was angry, her teeth gritted. She shoved me to the floor. 'You have no idea the pain you caused. I lost everything the day you were born.' It wasn't just anger anymore. It was sadness. Heartbreak. '*You* are the reason I had to become a Moon Whisperer.' She stopped herself. Held her tongue.

'You don't have to do this. I can help you – '

'I don't need your help. Once Lord Ellis takes your power, we'll rule this world. No more hiding in the shadows. No more surviving. No, we'll be living like Kings and Queens.'

'I'm sorry.' I rubbed my neck, breathed through the bruises. 'I'm sorry for the pain I caused you.'

Selene looked at me then, surprised. I thought I even saw her eyes soften, just a little. 'The only way I could hold onto the distant memory of what I'd lost was by joining your father out at sea. Surviving off our memories together... your apologies can't undo the last twelve years. I deserve more.' Selene drew her sword at me. 'Walk.' She demanded, but the question was on the tip of my tongue. If I dared to ask it. *You know where my father is?* 'I said walk!' She yelled. I scrambled to my feet.

Location: The Sovereign Palace, Tower

Selene guided me up the spiral stairs to the hexagonal room at the top of the leftmost tower. Inside, a tall, thin man stood in the centre of the room. He smiled a wicked smile at the sight of me. Selene shoved me towards him; I landed on my hands and knees at his feet.

'As per your request, my Lord.' Selene bowed.

'She's the spitting image of her mother.' He sounded disgusted at his own words.

'You're Lord Ellis?' I looked up at him, towering over me. In his hand, he held a staff with an orb. Inside, liquid blue swirled and sparkled. *Blue Magic.* 'You made the skies dark. The land die...'

'Well, aren't you intuitive?' He grimaced. 'I made my presence known, and with your help, I'm going to make Azzurra exactly what it was meant to be.'

'I won't help you.' I spat at his feet. He smacked me hard across the face without even thinking. I fell to the side. A tear in my eye. A tear I would not let fall. Not for him.

'It's sweet that you think you have a choice. Did I say sweet? I meant sickening.' He clenched his jaw and stared me down.

'What are you going to do to me?' My voice came out small, shaky. I realised then I was afraid. More afraid than I'd ever been.

'I'm going to drain you of your Scion Auras. Everything you have. Then I'm going to use them to rule Azzurra… after I've banished the rest of the Scions from existence, of course.' He laughed an evil laugh as my jaw dropped.

'But you can't –'

'Oh, but I am.' He shoved the Orbed staff to my throat and forced my head back. 'I will be the only power in this world, and the world will fall at my feet.' He hissed. I felt that tear trickle down my cheek. I blinked out two more. 'I have waited two decades for this moment. For a power to be born strong enough to create the world I deserve. I thought your mother would be enough, but she was cut short in her prime.' He dropped his staff and strode to the window. He yanked open the heavy curtains and let the shadowed light pour into the dark, dreary room illuminating the deep wood of the bookshelves that filled the wall. The light caught the gold of his cloak and reflected onto the light marble of the floor. Even the shine in his black hair lit up under the rays of the darkened sun. Past him, I could see the dragons that filled the sky for all their glory. They swarmed the clouds. Rings of fire shot through the black. Lord Ellis stepped out onto the small balcony and soaked in the misery he'd created. His arms outstretched, staff in one hand. 'Bring her.' He spoke loud and clear. Selene didn't hesitate; her hands were around my arm, pushing me forward. She thrust me out onto the balcony, and he planted the staff onto the marble ground between us. His eyes bore into mine. 'Take it.' He ordered me. I shook my head; I didn't have the nerve to speak. His mouth turned into an awful grimace, pure rage in his eyes. He stamped the staff down, demanding me to take hold. Selene grabbed my wrist and forced my hand. I fought as hard as I could, but I felt the warmth of the dragon scales on my palm. I screamed in anguish. It felt as though he was ripping my soul from me. The staff orb shone a bright blue, the skies swirled and morphed above us. I thought it would never end when suddenly his evil cackle stalled. He looked down at me, his brow furrowed deep. 'You said this would work!' He grunted at Selene, outraged.

'What's wrong?' Selene covered her face from the harsh wind around us with her other arm.

'It's not working. Her powers blocked. This can't be.' He jerked the staff about as if to kick start it again, but it was stuck. Selene, still holding my hand in place, looked between us, confused. I could still feel the pull of the orb, but it no longer hurt. He looked at me then as if examining me. 'Someone tied her magic….'

Selene looked at me; confusion filled her face. 'That's not possible. Only Blue Magic could that.' She breathed out, releasing my hand. I fell back as I was released from the orb's trance.

'You *said* this would be easy! You *said* I would have everything!' He cried out in a fury, swinging the staff. I ducked as it came towards me, and Selene was flung back into the room, a sparkle of blue around her. Lord Ellis was fuming now. He pointed the staff at me, but we both knew he had taken all that he could from me. 'Who did this to you?' He spat. I shook my head; I had no words. A million thoughts raced through my mind, but I couldn't settle on a single one. Fear coursed through me, overriding all other faculties. He breathed loud and heavy at me. The orb began to glow, magic shot out and hit me square in the chest. I rocketed back, hard, into the balcony wall. I hit the floor, gasping for air. It was like my lungs had stopped working. 'Who tied your magic?' His words were slow through gritted teeth. I forced myself to look up; To meet his eye. I pushed myself to my feet as he continued to stare me down. 'I will not lose this opportunity again. Tell me who's protecting you.' He pushed the staff towards me.

I immediately thought of Chief Eire, of Nuri, or Nook. They'd all protected me. I realised then what I was afraid of, and it wasn't Lord Ellis and what he could do to me. All I could think of was Nook. Cold. Hurt. In need of help. I felt a wave of strength come over me. I wouldn't let Lord Ellis take this world from us. They were wrong. Chief Eire, Nuri, even Nook, they had all been wrong. This *was* my fight.

I lunged at Lord Ellis. Hard. Fast. I connected with such force that we both barrelled over the edge of the balcony. His cries filled my ears as we fell through the sky. His staff turned in the air beside us as he desperately tried to reach for it. I could feel my heart in my chest as the ground neared us. The tears flew from my eyes as the wind carried them up and away, with the speed at which we fell. I should've been terrified. I should've felt the fear shoot through my veins; Felt the muscles in my body tense for impact.

Instead… I felt as though I could breathe… As if this entire time I had been holding my breath and now I was free… Free to think for myself and not be told who I am.

Time seemed to slow as I fell. Lord Ellis' face contorted as he screamed below me, still fumbling for his falling staff. I could see the entire city below me, from wall to wall. Around the city walls, an army was forming. I could see them in every direction. Chief Keahi's people rode in on horseback, armed and ready, followed by the mystical Da'go's of their land. Part deer, part spirit, entirely deadly. Chief Eire had enlisted every abled body from camp; they charged forward, shed of their fur coats, and armed in their battle gear. It looked as though most of Salt Glass City was present and aided by creatures of their sea, surviving on land through shared scions. Beings much resembling Eska, I could only assume was the Forré strode forward. I neared the ground now. What had once looked like ants, I could now see, were the CSC soldiers, equipped and ready to ward off the advancing army.

Time caught up, only metres from the ground. I heard the crunch and thump of Lord Ellis hitting the ground. His staff hit the ground; next, the glass orb shattered, releasing the Blue Magic it contained. His blood pooled around him as the magic exploded on impact. It clouded. Hovered around him for a moment as if thinking.

THWACK! I hit the ground. Pain ricocheted through every fibre of my body.

Part Four

Sometimes the sacrifices' we make are to

better the future not the present, and it's

not until that day comes that what seemed

selfish once was actually an act of

selflessness

Location: The Sovereign City Palace, Palace Square

I laid, paralysed on the concrete ground; Lord Ellis next to me, surrounded by his own blood. The cloud of magic made its decision. It flooded into me. I breathed it in; I felt whole. I hadn't realised the emptiness I'd felt with it gone. Then the sensation was gone, replaced by the searing pain burning throughout my body.

I looked ahead. I could feel the adrenaline and tension all around me; The war had begun. CSC soldiers stormed through the streets, firing at anything and everything that moved. I screamed in pain in my head as hands touched my back. I could hear the start of tears as Zosime turned me over. 'No, no, no, no, no.' She muttered to herself as her shaking hands stroked over my face. Her tears fell onto my chest. 'You can't die; this isn't how I saw it.' Her voice quivered. 'This isn't what I saw!' Her tears streamed down her cheeks. Behind her, in the sky, the flutter of wings. I looked past her to see Butternut, the sleeping pink faery from the woods. She hovered down, aligned herself over me, above Zosime. She examined me.

Such a small thing, to start such a big war. I heard Butternut's voice in my head. Sweet, lyrical.

Who am I? I pushed the question into Butternut's mind.

She came closer, then, *You're the dead princess we've all been waiting for.*

I felt a tear roll down my cheek. *But why?* I pushed the question as hard as I could.

'Hey!' Zosime looked back, sensing Butternut above us. 'Get away from her!' She shouted again, waving her away with her arms. Butternut swung back and up. Glided in the air.

'And what might you be?' Butternut spoke out loud to Zosime. Zosime gasped as Butternut swooped down towards her, just out of reach. 'You're… *peculiar*. Not true-blooded. Who made you?' Butternut spoke, malice in her voice, now. Zosime stumbled for a reply when a glass dagger shot through the air. Butternut squealed in anguish. THUMP! She hit the floor in front of me. She was distraught, crying. Her wings floated down beside her. Sliced, clean off. She screamed again at the sight of them. Nuri sprinted towards her from across the square. Zosime threw the glass dagger back towards him. He grabbed it as he pinned the faery to the floor in front of me. Zosime, legs shaking, cheeks still wet with tears, she bent down over me once more, kissed my forehead, I saw the glow of purple on her hand, and she whispered, 'You'll never be alone.' She took a final look at me before sprinting away.

'What are you doing here? You're not allowed this far out.' Nuri questioned Butternut angrily, his hand around her throat, holding her to the ground with little force.

'Didn't you hear? We're at war, *little prince*.' Butternut replied through a strained voice. A menacing smile followed. She turned to look me in the eye as he held her more forcefully. *Sometimes, destruction must reign for peace to rise up.* Even in my head, her voice was strained. Weak.

Butternut's eyes widened as Nuri sliced her throat clean through. I felt my heart jump at the sight. I watched the life fade from her eyes and the magic seep from her fingertips back into the world. She was gone. Nuri's attention was on me then. He rushed to me. I felt his hand on my shoulder.

'Aveline.' He stroked my hair, bent down to meet my eye. I felt him then. Nook was close. I smiled with relief inside; it was like a weight off my chest; he was okay. I took a deep breath, the purple circle started to glow. I was with him.

I could see what Nook saw. Feel what he felt. He was in the middle of the battle. I was beside him again like a hallucination. Dust filled the air around him as buildings protected friend and enemy alike. Soldiers let out shot after shot. Bolts of energy flew through the air. Arrows and spears pierced through armour and skin as though it were rice paper, tearing lines of blood. Followed by the cries of pain. Glass blades sliced upwards, ripping souls from their chests as yet more soldiers fell to the ground. While around them, people ran, hiding in the nearest buildings, shielding children from the chaos that was building. Spurts of blue blood rose through the air as the creatures howled in pain, tails striking out and teeth piercing flesh. 'Aveline?' Nook saw me there beside him, wavering in and out. I beamed with delight to see him, his face had been bandaged, and he looked good as new.

I'm here.

Where? He dodged and ducked the oncoming slaughter of CSC soldier attacks. Ahead Chief Eire was taking on multiple combatants at once. Graceful. Agile. Lethal.

In the Palace square. I'm fine. Just be careful. I told him as a soldier's blast missed him by mere millimetres. I saw Eos then; she was swift with a battle stick. Her white sleeves, already soaked in blood. She took out a CSC soldier as his gun aimed towards Chief Eire.

I'm coming to you. Nook thrust his dagger deep into the belly of a man twice his size without a second thought. Ripped it out again, the blood warm on his skin.

No! They need you here. I'll find you after. I hoped I didn't sound as desperate as I felt.

Aveline wait! I heard him call as I faded away.

I could see Nuri again; he wiped the tear that fell from my eye. 'I'm going to get you help.' He told me softly; sadness radiated from him. He didn't even know me, and when he looked at me, helpless, on the floor, it was like he was breaking. He looked around desperately, only to see desert dust coating the air. It blinded all but the smallest of the Forré who shot through the crowds, shooting poison darts, into the uniformed legs of the attackers. While the agile bodies of their urban legends pounced beside them, two more appeared to rise for every soldier that fell. Nuri darted back, shielded me with his body, as out of nowhere came the hum of machines. The dragons were no longer the sole bearers of the skies. Drones zoomed through the sky, blasting down over the city, taking out corners of buildings, rubble tumbling down, crushing anyone in its path. More soldiers flew alongside them in SkySearchers shooting down through the dust without clear sight as to who was below.

'NURI!' a voice shot through the dust. A woman from Salt Glass City appeared through the cloud, darting towards us.

'Benalla.' Nuri greeted her as she knelt at my side.

'Is she alive?' She asked Nuri, while looking at me.

'Barely. We need Castalia. Where is she?' He asked as they both ducked out of the way of a series of blasts in our direction.

'I'll find her, but Nuri,' She placed a hand on his arm, 'River never turned up to fight.' Worry filled her eyes as she spoke. 'No one's seen him.' They both looked at me then.

'Go. Go find Castalia. If we can't save Aveline, everything will have been for nothing anyway.' He pushed her away, and she ran fast back into the throng of the battle.

'AVELINE!' Nook's broken voice cried through the settling cloud of dust. Another tear fell down my cheek as he came into view. I felt his heart pounding. His breath caught, unable to exhale as he raced to me. He skidded to a stop, stumbling over his own feet in his desperation to get to me. 'Aveline?' Tears welled in his eyes. Nuri's hand was on his shoulder, the only thing holding him together. 'Aveline…' he breathed. His shaking hand brushed the hair from my face. 'Aveline.' He choked. I tried to stay silent. I tried to sever our connection. I wanted to spare him the hope that I might survive. His agony was too much. I could feel it ripping through my soul and pouring out of my heart.

I'm here. I'm here, Nook. I pushed the thought as he wrapped his blood-spattered hand around my icy cold one.

'You said you were fine.' He whispered.

'HELP!' A piercing scream tore through our eardrums. Nook and Nuri both looked past me.

'Alillia.' Nuri breathed. He jumped to his feet and took off.

What happened?

'Lady Alillia, she's been stabbed.' He told me. I let myself go again and pushed into Nook's mind. I could see what he saw. Nuri grabbed a bleeding woman just as she fell to the ground. Her light blue silk, stained with still pulsing blood. He held her in his arms on the floor, pushed down on her wound. Her bloodied hand over his. Her cheeks, puffy, wet with tears. Behind them, slinking away from the Palace, was Captain Azaevior. He had his gun drawn, but I didn't have the strength to hold on any longer; I could feel myself fading away; I was losing feeling all over.

'No. Hold on, Aveline. We can save you.' Nook squeezed my hand tighter. My already weak breath was taken away at the sight of the dark green-furred beast approaching. Its eyes, just as hypnotic as they'd been in the woods. It moved slowly. Purposefully.

Nook… I used what was left of my energy to warn him. He spun fast, didn't hesitate before stretching himself to shield me. Still, the beast came. I could see Nook's hand quiver in front of my face. The other held his dagger out in front of him, warning the beast away. Then, a furred hand shot into my eye line, grabbed Nook by the wrist and pulled him away. I heard him yelp as he landed on the hard concrete.

'What are you doing?' His voice was sharp, livid. There was nothing between the beast and me now.

'Don't look it in the eye.' A woman's voice, shouted.

'Castalia, let me go!' Nook fought her off. The beast continued slowly towards me.

'It will kill you.' Castalia replied.

'It will kill her!' He snapped.

The beast was on top of me now. Its front paws pressed down on my shoulders. Its weight pushing me down into the stone ground. Its breath, hot, wet, on my skin. It curled its lips back, bared its jagged jaw. My vision started to blackout. I tried desperately to keep them open. I felt its fur on my cheek as it lowered its head and bit down. I felt the sharp pain of its pointed teeth sink deep around my shoulder. I felt nothing but searing pain. The world blacked out around me. It felt as though it would never end. I wasn't even sure I was alive anymore. Then a cooling sensation spread through my veins. I felt weightless. Then I began to tingle, head to toe, my blood began to pulse again. The beast released me from its jaw. I slowly opened my eyes to see it looking down at me; I smiled and brought my hand to its face. I blinked away the blurriness as I let out my first breath, and the beast leapt away. Disappeared into the chaos that was still unfolding around us without even a look back.

I laid, looking up at the firey, dragon-filled sky. The dark clouds had begun to part; ash and dust rained down over us now. Nook's face abruptly filled my view. His hands, on my shoulders. Slowly, with his help, I sat up. We sat, staring at each other while all around us, blood continued to fill the streets of The Soveriegn City.

'Are you okay?' Nook finally said. He brushed the messy curls away from my face and looked down at the blood dripping from my shoulder. His hand slipped into mine as he pulled away. *Never do that again.*

I squeezed his hand tight. *Never*

Castalia approached us cautiously. She wasn't much taller than either of us. Deerlike in appearance. Delicate features. Brown and white colouring. 'What *was* that thing?' Nook looked at her.

'It was a creature of myth.' She replied, still staring after where it had disappeared. 'It was told there was a creature that could put you in a trance; it would rip you limb from limb without causing you so much as a whisper.' She continued. 'But, the mythical part, it had the ability to heal. It could give life as freely as it took it, but it would only heal those it considered to be as formidable as itself.' She and Nook both looked to me then, but I was looking past them to Lady Alillia, still bleeding out in Nuri's arms. Castalia followed my gaze and rushed over to try and help. I looked around at the destruction enclosing us; It felt as though it would never cease. Nook at my side, knowing our thoughts were the same. *What is this solving?*

'It was too easy….' I said, looking at Lord Ellis' body. 'To stop him, it was all too easy-' I stopped abruptly at the sight of a creature with fur whiter than snow, wings faster than any bird and scales under its fur so tough; not even the blades of Salt Glass City could penetrate its heart, gliding elegantly over the city towards us. The same beast that had charged at Nook in the Pink Mountains. On his back, *'Eska?'* my mouth dropped open, and Nook turned to look too. As it neared, we saw a girl was riding with him. The great creature rolled as it approached; the girl leapt from its back and rolled to a stop towards us as the winged beast soared gracefully through the sky into the eye of the dragon's tornado under Eska's command. Nook raised a fist in cheer, hollered out as Eska soared the beast upwards. WHOOSH! The girl released a spear that rocketed past us and straight into the heart of a CSC soldier that had snuck up behind us. She straightened, proud of her accomplishment and looked to us both.

'Is she okay?' The girl asked Nook about me. Nook nodded. The girl crossed her hand from left to right across her shoulders and then to her forehead. Nook mirrored the gesture. 'Take her, hide now. Chief's orders.' She told us as she sprinted past to retrieve her spear from the dead soldier's chest. The battle had been spurred on once more. Nook didn't hesitate; he grabbed my wrist and pulled me to my feet.

We ran through the streets, dodging gunfire and crumbling buildings. I slipped on blood-soaked stones, and Nook steadied me as we continued to sprint through the battleground until we reached a small tailor shop. We leapt up the stairs and through the unlocked door. Nook dragged me through the darkened shop to the small room at the back, piled high with clothes. We slumped down the wall, our backs to the front of the shop. Our breathing, heavy. Nook's hand firmly in mine. I turned my head to face him. 'Chief Keahi's niece, Naeva. He ordered your protection by his people, for your mother.' He answered my question before I could ask it. My mouth dropped open slightly.

'My mother?'

'Chief said she visited him, not long after King Petri's death-'

I cut him off as it dawned on me, 'If we'd gone to the Arid land like you said if I'd listened to you, we would've seen her-' Suddenly Nook's arms were around me. He held me tight as if letting me go would make me fall apart. I held on, too, as if he really were keeping me together.

'No one's winning here, Nook.' I whispered. We both flinched as the building around us shook, gunfire raining down.

'I know. At least Lord Ellis is gone now. His soldiers will fall too.' He got to his feet, pulled me with him.

I shook my head. 'There was a girl with a purple Scion Aura. Another Oracle…' I said, still in slight disbelief.

'That's how they knew how to find us… to find you?' Nook realised, that no matter where we had gone, we would never have been safe. 'You were right, about fighting and not hiding.' He finsihed, slighty ashamed.

I shook my head, *We didn't know.*

You knew…

'I don't think she worked for Lord Ellis. She took care of me. Worried about me. ' I told him, moving on from our dwelling, there was no time. I thought back to how Selene had treated Zosime, to how she'd cried thinking I would die. 'Have you ever heard of Zosime?'

Nook's mouth dropped open. He was about to speak when a trap door crashed open, the rug on top flying back. A boy, not much older than us, sprang out of the hole in the floor determinedly and took in the room.

'*You?*' Nook said, surprised. I looked between them, both confused.

'You must be the dead girl everyone's so excited about.' He turned to me; Nook immediately stepped in front, guarding me.

'You said you weren't after her.' Nook spat.

You know him? I grabbed Nook's sleeve, scrunched it between my fingers. He nodded in reply.

'Rune.' The boy said, looking between us quizzically, 'And I'm not, but it's always fun to meet someone that's supposed to be dead.' He wiggled his eyebrows, acting as if we weren't in the middle of a war. 'Did I hear the name Zosime?' He stepped forward curiously, holding my eye. I nodded.

'What do you want with her?' I stepped out beside Nook, still holding his sleeve.

'Just to find her. I came in search of her; we think she might be in trouble.'

'We?' Nook asked; I could feel his hand poised to reach for the dagger in his boot.

'Another came with me to bring her home.' Rune replied.

'Lydia?' Nook asked, curious now, his defences lowering as Rune nodded in reply.

'How long was I *out* for?' I asked him, confused. It seemed he'd had a whole adventure without me.

'A lot happened, *fast*.' He replied quickly. We all ducked suddenly as something significant crashed through the building opposite; the impact blasted through the glass in the front door and scattered into the shop. Dust clouded in after it. We looked out to see a CSC drone impaled into the building on fire and smoking. Crash after crash followed around us. Rune strode confidently to the front door to investigate.

'Wait!' I grabbed Rune's sleeve and tugged him back. 'Are you insane? You can't go out there!'

He smiled at me, almost laughed as if I were being dramatic. 'Look at that, the world crumbling around you, and you're worried about me.' He took my hand, stroked down my palm, the blue circle appeared, he turned his palm over, it appeared on his too. My mouth dropped open. He breathed in as if soaking in the magic. 'Thanks for that.'

'How did you-' I started, but he poofed away in a cloud of blue.

'What just happened?' I turned to Nook. He shook his head silently. 'Did you know you could steal Scion

Aura's?' I asked, looking at my now empty palm. Nook shook his head again.

'You said Zosime had your Orcale Scion?' He asked, taking my hand, examining it as if it had the answers on it.

'Not *mine*, she just had one too....' I took my hand away. 'Who's Lydia?'

'Another stranger. She came with Nuri to Light Creek Cove after you disappeared. He didn't seem to trust her.'

'You've never seen them before?' I asked, curious, it was a big world, but most people were identifiable, especially to the rulers of the lands. Nook shook his head in reply. We both shared a fearful look.

Outside, the rumbling had stopped. There was a noticeable quiet in the air.

Location: The Sovereign City, Palace Square

The tension had fallen, a sense of awe spread across the

battle. When we reached the Palace Square once more,

we saw why. I released the breath I didn't know I was

holding as, one by one, the dragons dropped from the

sky. They fell into line behind Eska's mythical beast,

who circled the city until nothing but the dragons'

coloured scales could be seen as a blur of bright colours in the sky. The rush of wind stopped the people in their tracks as their heavy wings' pushed the gust of air downwards with every stroke. The CSC drones tore from the sky, knocked from the city grounds by the great beasts and crashed in puddles of smoke and flames. Nook and I ducked behind a crumbled wall of a building. We watched in awe, unable to do anything but watch as the Kingdom destroyed itself from within The Sovereign City walls. Faster and faster, they fell, swallowed in puddles of fire, and ripped from the earth by the swirl of thick dust.

Across the square, we saw Chief Eire; she held Eos at her side. She was injured. Bleeding. They both found us in the crowd, looked at us, sat amongst the final moments of the battle. By the Palace, Benalla was at

Nuri's side, trying to stop the bleeding that poured from Lady Alillia's wound. Butternut maimed and slaughtered beside Lord Ellis in the middle of the square.

Slowly, one by one, weapons' fell to the ground, lost in the debris of their fallen, their eyes searching the destruction. Blood stricken walls, faces of anguish surrounding the sorrow they felt. Hand in hand, they gathered their own, the survivors of their horror. Departing from the crumbled and cracked walls, group by group until all that remained were the ghosts of what they once knew. Naeva spotted us crouched behind the dusty rubble and hurtled through the dismayed crowd towards us. She was breathing hard, blood-spattered down her clothes, across her skin. Her spear, still in her hand. We got to our feet as she arrived. Nook embraced her with a warm hug, which she gratefully received. She turned to me next. 'It's lovely to meet you, Aveline.' She extended her bloodied hand. I took it graciously.

'Thank you for saving us.' I dipped my head, unsure of the hierarchy I stood in.

Naeva looked unsure like she shouldn't speak what was on her mind. 'You should know, the rulers are all on edge.' She said, her eyes focused on me. 'With Blue Magic released, You *and* your mother returning from the dead.'

'We weren't really dead.' I replied softly.

'Duchess Astraea didn't turn up to fight. They're starting to talk.' Naeva continued. She wasn't trying to be mean. It felt more like a warning. 'We came with loyalty to her, to The Sovereign's. To save you.'

'Duchess?' I asked quickly

Confused, Naeva replied, 'Your mother-'

'My mother is the *Duchess* of The Sovereign City?' The words fell from my mouth. I looked to Nook; he was just as surprised.

'You didn't think this many people turned up to fight for just anyone, did you, Aveline?'

'Naeva!' Chief Keahi's voice bellowed across the square. We all looked to see him beckoning her over, to join the rest of his people return to their land.

'I have to get back to help with the wounded. Be careful Aveline, I don't know why, but everyone is very afraid that you're here.'

'People do unpredictable things when they're scared.' Nook finished. Naeva nodded, a small sigh. She kissed Nook on the cheek, then they both gestured left to right, shoulder and to their foreheads. She smiled at me sadly before she darted into the remnants of the war.

'What is that you do?'

'It's a sign the Arid use of thanks and goodbye and respect as it's needed.' Nook replied, but he was distracted, 'Was that really the only thing you picked up from that conversation?' He raised a brow at me.

'It's the only thing I can begin to understand.' I confessed. I couldn't process what Naeva had just said. How could I be so terrifying to so many people? I looked to Nook, but he was already scanning the beaten-down crowd.

'You're looking for that boy, Rune, aren't you?'

Nook nodded. 'He knows more about Azzurra than we do. If the adults aren't going to tell us what's going on, maybe he will.'

'He'll be with Zosime.'

'Where is she?'

I shrugged in reply. I hadn't seen her since she'd left me paralysed on the floor. He looped his arm in mine as we looked across the devastation in front of us. Chief Eire and Eos were helping the wounded people of the Pink Mountains. Castalia was with Lady Alillia, Benalla, helping her inside.

'Can you feel it?' Nook stopped and looked to the skies. I knew what he was talking about. I hadn't stopped feeling it; it had grown stronger with every hour of the day.

'Blue Magic.' I breathed.

'It's spreading, growing; whoever was controlling Lord Ellis might not be so easy to beat.' We both inhaled deeply at the thought; our eyes drifted to the bloodied stone where I had laid paralysed and dying.

'They had a plan. One that used Lord Ellis as a pawn. Killed King Petri.'

'And put you on everyone's map.' Nook finished. 'What do they want?' He asked openly. We didn't have an answer. We stood in silence for a moment. I played back the events of the last few hours in my head. Lord Ellis, on the balcony. *Selene.* 'What, what is it?' Nook turned me to face him.

'Selene. She was the one that kidnapped me.'

'For Lord Ellis. We already know this wasn't his-'

'No.' I cut him off. 'She told him how to take my power. He was going on *her* word.' I continued, trying to work out the rest of the puzzle in my head, but nothing was quite fitting together. I exhaled, disappointed.

'It's okay.' He took my hand, held it tight. 'We'll figure it out. The important thing is that you're safe for now.' He smiled, relieved. I nodded, but there was still a fear growing in the pit of my stomach.

'It's in me, Nook. I can feel it.' I held his eye; I couldn't hide the fear in mine, but his remained steady, calm.

'Blue Magic? Of course, you do.' He smiled, 'Scions are powered by Blue Magic, you know that.'

'Right, of course, they are. That's completely normal.' I shook my bad feeling away, but Lord Ellis' words repeated in my head, '*Someone tied her magic…*'. There was more in me that I couldn't reach yet. More than the Scions I'd already conjured, more than the blue cloud of smoke that made me disappear, and someone in Azzurra knew it too. *Did they want to protect me or use me?*

Location: The Sovereign City, City Square

Nook and I walked side by side down the wrecked streets of the Sovereign City back to the Palace. Lord Ellis was sent to be burnt beyond recognition to avoid any chance of his return from the dead. Those that were left of the CSC soldiers were sentenced to life on Dragon Isle. The prison I'd recently learnt Lord Ellis had served time in at the request of his brother, the late King Petri,

only days after I had supposedly died. Selene hadn't been

located yet. Captain Azaeviour was on the run, last seen

heading for the dark woods. No one else had even heard

of Zosime or Rune, but they'd definitely caught their

interest. Eska's white-furred saviour had led the dragons

back to their home on Dragon Isle; those of them that

hadn't survived the battle were flown back in the

clutches of their comrades' talons. Everyone else had

begun the journey back to their homelands. Citizens hid

behind their closed doors. Tails disappeared back into

the dark ocean, snowy footsteps vanished into the Pink

Mountains, and a trail of dusty sand could be followed

back to the Arid. Nuri accompanied us, wanting to see

the extent of the damage himself. I could tell his heart

sank every time we passed the body of one of his fallen.

Their scales no longer shined and glimmered their rose gold; they were now dull, lifeless. 'It should never have come to this.' He wiped his mouth, swallowing the emotion that was rising as he knelt over what was left of one of his companions.

'Sometimes, destruction must reign for peace to rise up.' I repeated the words Butternut had pushed into my mind. I was as surprised I'd said them as Nuri and Nook were.

'Unfortunately, I think this is only the beginning.' Nuri replied solemnly.

We looked across the debris and death before us. The street, lined with broken buildings, scorched ground, and bloody stains so deep the stones looked as if they'd been painted. Nook bent down over a small, orange furred, large-eared creature's body. It was the same as Goldie, but instead of poison, its tail was flamed.

'So, many creatures I'd heard stories of from the Elders. I never knew they were real.' He said as he stroked down the silky fur of the creature that no longer breathed. 'They defended us. Fought at our side.' Nuri traced the outline of a dead havsvarg nearby. 'They knew we needed them….'

A woman from Salt Glass City approached from ahead. She bowed at Nuri, then Nook. 'Karratha?' Nuri got to his feet. She looked unsure. Upset.

'I have news from Salt Glass City….' She started but couldn't bring herself to finish. Tears began to well in her eyes. Nuri couldn't imagine what she wanted to say. He couldn't allow that thought to even cross his mind; it was so awful. Karratha's lip began to quiver under the weight of the words that had to come out.

'She's dead, isn't she?' I broke the silence. Everyone looked at me.

'Alillia?' Nuri gasped. Karratha stared back at him, wishing it had been. Nook looked to me, and he knew.

'Her Majesty of Salt Glass City.' Nook announced. Nuri looked at him in shock. It was as if we could see his heart stop beating for a second.

'Your mother's body was found on the edge of Salt Glass Lake …' Karratha managed to explain, grateful we'd taken most of the burden. Nuri dropped to his knees. Eyes blank. He sank back onto his feet. 'She was murdered.' Karratha's voice cracked. Her hand to her mouth. Nook and I stared at her, dumbfounded.

Lord Ellis was here for the entire battle… I looked at Nook.

He really was a pawn in someone else's game.

But who's? I frowned, a pit of concern growing in my stomach. Then I remembered what the faery had said to Nuri, *'Didn't you hear? We're at war, little prince.'*

'Triden found her; he heard her last words.' Karratha swallowed.

'She saw who attacked her?' Nuri was suddenly on his feet again, ready for action. Karratha looked at me; there was a spark of fear in her eyes.

'He said her last word was, *Astraea*.' She forced herself to look back at Nuri, but he'd turned to look at me. I stared back, confused.

'Astraea was with us; she built this uprising.' Nuri looked back to Karratha, expecting more evidence to her words.

'She also didn't turn up to fight, nor did River.' She looked back at me now.

My father? I looked to Nook. He was already stepping beside me, his fingers looped around mine. He shrugged gently.

Nuri shook his head, 'Then maybe she knows who's vying for power. Maybe she's in trouble.'

'I'll send out a search for her?' Karratha asked timidly. He looked back at her as if questioning why she was asking him. 'You're in charge now, *King* Nuri?' She tipped her head to bow. Nuri looked taken aback. He hadn't had the time to process what his mother's death had truly meant. He took a moment to think.

'Gather the rulers to the Sovereign Palace. It's time we shared what little we know.' He ordered Karratha. 'I want someone at Lady Alillia's side; the moment she wakes, I want to know… we still don't know who attacked her.' He nodded decisively. Karratha hurried away.

Nuri's eyes were on me.

Location: Sovereign City Palace, Palace Gardens

Azzurra had begun to heal already. The sky was blue.

The clouds, white. The earth, soft. The gardens were just

as I had imagined they would be when I looked out of

the window. Colourful. Thriving. Perfectly kept. The

perfect place to walk on a sunny day, and a sunny day it

was. I sat with Nook on the hand-carved bench in the

middle of the gardens. Surrounded by the song of the

birds and the smell of freshly cut flowers.

'I don't see why we weren't allowed to be in there.'

Nook sulked, slumping back into the bench. Across from

us, Goldie was sniffing through the foliage. Scratching at

the loose pebbles in the gravel.

'They don't think kids can be helpful.' I told him,

staring at the glass doors that led into the Palace

Conference room where the rulers of the lands were

debating about what to do next. The Sovereign City was

still in tatters. Everyone had taken a loss on their

population, and trust had utterly broken down.

'Well, I guess technically, you did start a war.' Nook

laughed.

'I did no such thing.' I shoved him so hard he

toppled off the bench. There was an awkward silence

because we both knew deep down that I wasn't an innocent bystander in all this. 'No one blames you.' He slid back onto the bench.

'Maybe they should. It was rather selfish of me to come back from the dead and disrupt the peace.' A small smile at the corners of my mouth. Nook laughed again.

'I don't think we were at peace.' He said as he walked over to the blue petalled flowers on the shrub. 'I think we were asleep. Content with living our separate lives, too afraid to say it wasn't right.' He chose carefully, plucked the prettiest flower from the bunch, 'We were held together by inked signatures and the fear of stepping out of line.' He walked back and placed the blue flower in my hair, just as he had before.

'And now?' I asked, touching the delicate petals as he sat down again.

'Now, we have the chance to start again. To come together, forget the old ways. Stop pretending that because no one said it was wrong, that made it right.'

'I told you you'd make a good Chief one day.' I pulled the flower from my hair. Held it between us. 'You have to make a wish.' I told him. 'Whoever pulls the last petal, their wish comes true.' I said, plucking the first one. He immediately plucked the next, then I, then him until there was only one left. We both went for it. As his hand touched mine, my breath was caught, my palm purple. I felt the warm breeze through my hair, acoustic music in my ears and the silky sand beneath my feet and beside me,

'Aveline?' Nook's voice broke through. I blinked away the future and focused on Nook. 'What was it this time?'

'Hopefully, a wish coming true.' I smiled at him. Looked at the petal still in our hands. I plucked it.

'Aveline?' A woman's voice pulled us back into reality. I turned to see Lady Alillia. She looked weak, still hurt but bandaged. Nook immediately got to his feet and bowed.

'My Lady.' He held his hand out to her, she shook it politely. I got to my feet too; I began to bow when she stopped me.

'There's no need for that.' She smiled and extended her hand to me. I took it and stepped closer to her. She just looked at me for a moment as if she were trying to remember every second. Then, finally, with a wince, she pulled a velvet pouch from her pocket. 'I have never regretted a decision so much in my life as I did when I betrayed your mother.' She turned the velvet pouch out in my hands, and a gold necklace fell out. It had three gold circles, one beneath each other on a chain. She placed it around my neck; it felt heavy as it glinted in the sunlight. 'These will get you whatever you may need.' She said as she pushed one of the circles, it spun around within its holder. I looked closer to see one side had an engraving of a large 'A' and the other an engraving of The Sovereign Palace. 'Use them wisely, Aveline. Whoever you may trade them too will then be able to bargain them further.'

'Azzurian Gold coins.' Nook breathed, staring at them. 'The Elders of the Pink Mountains spoke of them.' He looked up at Lady Alillia with awe. 'Most were lost to the bottom of the ocean when the Moon Whisperers' were cast out.'

'Most, but not all.' She smiled. I didn't share their awe and amazement. There was only one part of that conversation that had caught my attention.

'You betrayed my mother?'

Lady Alillia looked down at me with deep regret. 'I was young. Jealous. I never thought-'

'Do you know where she is?' I asked, a little too hopeful. Lady Alillia shook her head.

'Until today, I thought she was dead. As were you.' She stroked down my hair. 'Now I fear the next time I see her; it'll be in cold blood.' She looked tearful now. 'She's a force your mother, one that tends to explode on impact.' She didn't seem to be able to help herself then. She reached down through the pain in her side and hugged me tight. I had that sensation again, but this wasn't a vision. Not a window into the past; it was a feeling that reached through every fibre of my being. It was wholesome and pained. It ached, but it warmed me. It made me want to laugh and scream. It was love in its truest form. The good despite the bad. I let out a deep exhale as she pulled away from me.

'She loves you. Despite everything. My mother loves you.' I told her softly. She broke into the widest grin. Tears down her cheeks.

'Thank you, Aveline.'

A throat clearing snapped all our heads towards the Palace. It was Nuri; he looked solemn as he walked towards us. Lady Alillia wiped the tears quickly away and straightened up. I tucked the necklace behind my top before turning all the way to face him.

'My Lady.' Nuri half bowed. Lady Alillia mirrored him. 'You should be resting.' He told her.

She nodded and glanced down at me. 'Remember, once something is set in motion, it will only build momentum. It is better to follow its direction than fight against it.' She smiled and left.

Nuri turned to me and held out his hand. 'I need you to come with me.'

'Where?' I asked.

'It's been decided that you pose an imminent threat to whoever is harbouring you.'

'She would never hurt –' Nook began to defend me, but Nuri cut him off.

'Whoever is trying to take control of Azzurra has made it clear they are willing to shed any amount of blood to attain the power she possesses.'

'And what else?' I crossed my arms. He looked at me just as Chief Eire did when I knew something I wasn't supposed to.

Nuri sighed before answering. 'Both of your parents are missing. There is, question, as to what role they played-'

'They are *not* evil-'

'We don't have the support to prove they're not with malicious intent.' Nuri snapped. He was angry, but not at me. At the situation. 'Do you have any idea where they are?' His voice softened now. I shook my head; he believed me. 'I've ordered a T-Pod to take you to Light Creek Cove. You're to stay there while we find out how big a threat we're dealing with.'

'She's a sitting duck there!' Nook exclaimed.

'Everyone else is a sitting duck if she's near them.' Nuri told him. Chief Eire and Eos came through the large glass doors from the conference room. 'The Chief and your mother have allowed you to say goodbye.' Nuri continued. Nook looked to his parents across the gardens. Then to me. He was torn.

I said I'd never leave you. I heard Nook's thoughts clear as day. Chief Eire looked grave as they approached. She looked to Nuri; he nodded once. Then, he gestured for Nook to leave with him. Nook was reluctant at first, but he gave in and followed Nuri down the path out of earshot.

'Aveline,' Chief Eire started, but she didn't know how to finish her sentence; she stepped forward, took both of my hands in hers, 'When you were born, I promised your mother I would protect you like you were my own. Now I'm asking that you let me protect my son from the evil we've shielded you from.' She stroked her thumbs across the back of my hands. 'Do you understand what I'm asking?'

I looked at Nook, swallowed. I looked back to Chief Eire's pain-filled eyes. Slowly, I nodded. She took my face in her hands and kissed the top of my head. 'What did she promise you?' My heart was in my stomach. I understood now, every good deed came with strings attached. No one did anything out of the goodness of their hearts.

'You're a smart girl Aveline. I fear the day you discover your true power.'

'The day my spark scorches the earth?'

Chief Eire took her hands away and stepped back beside Eos. She had been bandaged since the battle, but she wasn't at full strength. 'We know you'd never consciously cause him harm.' Eos began, her eyes flicking to Nook and back. 'But he is all we have, and we cannot put him in the danger that's following you.' I knew she was trying to show sympathy. To try and make it okay, but nothing would make Nook hating me, make it okay. I knew he'd follow me, so did they. He already had. Chief Eire and Eos stepped away. Nook walked back; Nuri watched from afar. He knew what they had asked me to do.

'Don't worry, I'll find a way to get to you. You won't be alone for long.' Nook told me quietly. A glance at his parents as he did.

'I don't want you to.' I told him. It was like a wave of grief hit me. My insides ached.

'What are you talking about?' His voice was small, hurt.

'I don't want you to follow me. I don't want you around.' Every word burnt my mouth. I could feel his heart cracking. His blood pulsing. 'You're not my family.' I forced the words to sound angry. 'My family is out there waiting for me. You've been a distraction. Keeping me from them.' I was going to cry; I could feel it. I shoved him with everything I had. He fell back hard, he couldn't catch himself, he hit the gravelled ground and skidded back. 'I don't *need* you.' I finished, my hands balled at my sides, all my emotion channelled into them. I couldn't let him see me break. I had to make him believe.

He stared back at me with the saddest eyes. I could feel the weight of his pain in my chest; he was so confused. So, hurt. I wanted to reach out to him. To hug him. To tell him everything would be okay. I couldn't hold it any longer; the tears fell.

'I hate you, Nook.' I ran. I had to get away from his pain. I couldn't bear it. It was crushing me. Goldie was hot on my heels, tiny paws working double-time to keep up with me. Nuri chased behind, his long legs bridging the gap faster than I wanted. I heard his heavy footsteps on the gravel behind me. Still, I didn't stop. I ran through the garden hedges, through the Palace Square and finally, at the gates to the Palace, I fell. I dropped to my knees.

I had nothing left; my tears were dry.

My heart, broken.

Nuri's footsteps stopped running at the sight of me. He slowed into a walk. Allowed me, to just be. I fell back into the wall, slumped against it. Goldie nuzzled into my limp arm. Then, after a moment, Nuri bent down and scooped me up like a parent would a child. 'How could you make me do that?' I breathed.

'Because it was the right thing to do.' He replied.

'Then why does it hurt so much?'

Nuri paused before answering me. When he did, he spoke slowly, as if thinking about every word. 'Sacrificing something you love to protect another is never without pain, but it does require a strength not everyone has.'

Location: Light Creek Cove, Lighthouse

I sat in the dimly lit room. Goldie staring at me from the
other end of the sofa. Our tubs of Squigglepop, still on
the table. The half-drunk teacup, still by the window. I
looked out to see, night had fallen; not even the stars
could light the darkness I felt inside. I looked around at
the mess. The discarded blankets. The books. I started

with the tubs. Put them in the bin in the kitchen, the forks in the sink. The blankets, folded on the sofa. I went to the teacup next. The china, cool to the touch, but it was outweighed by the past as my hand glowed purple. The teacup, now in my mother's hand as she sat on the window seat. I watched in awe, the memory clear as day, clearer than any other had been.

'How long are we going to do this?' My mother's voice came out soft as she placed the teacup down, exactly where I'd picked it up. Beside her was a man. My father? I could feel it, the love she felt for him. The same love Nuri felt for her. She leant her head into his shoulder, and they stared out the window to the glittering stars above.

'Do what?' My father replied, tightening his arm slightly as my mother shifted her weight in his arms.

'Pretend as though this can be our life….' My mother sighed and pushed away from him, shuffling to sit against the window seat wall. Her dark dress draped over the side, pooling on the floor. He sat down opposite her, his foot on the seat between them. She leant forward as he took her hands, and they rested on his knee. His CSC jacket fell over her wrist, much too big on her small frame.

CSC? I thought, shocked. He can't be my father… She wouldn't…

'Why can't it? Why can't we have this one happiness?' He replied, stroking her hand with his thumb.

'Because unfortunately, as much as we want to, we don't live in our dreams, and one day we're going to have to step back into reality.'

'Says who?' He smiled that dreamers smile that warmed her heart. 'Who, says we have to live in reality? Perhaps reality is for those who can't dream of anything better. A blank canvas for those yet to learn how to paint,'

'River,'

*River? He **was** my father. It couldn't be. The enemy? I felt myself step back away from them. My head shaking.*

'I'm serious; let's do this. Let's make our own reality, one where we get to choose. One where we get to sit beneath the stars every night and imagine the possibilities of the world.' He pulled her to her feet and into the small space between the window and the sofa.

'Tell me,'

'Tell you what?' She replied, beginning to smile as his arm slid around her waist, and they began to dance.

'Tell me what you want, we're painting our life, what do you want to see in that picture?' River swept her around gracefully back and forth past the window smiling as she bit her lip.

'I want laughter,' she smiled as he spun her under his arm.

'Good, what else?'

'Sunshine,'

'Keep going,' he said, lifting her into the air and elegantly back onto the wooden floor, bracing her in his arms again.

'Unbelievably good food,' she laughed,

'Bigger!'

'A house, not too big, something cosy,' she beamed,

'More! Something you really want...' he slowed their pace almost to a stop until he was just holding her up as they swayed.

'I want you,' she dropped her hands from his shoulders into his hands between them. 'I want you, and I want a little version of you and me, and I want us to be a family...' she whispered as her eyes glazed over.

Unconsciously I had moved closer to my mother; I was standing staring up at her. So, close I could hear her breathing.

'But we can't have that....' My mother dropped her head and breathed away the tears.

'Duchess Astraea of Azzurra,' River spoke calmly, steady. I felt my eyes widen as my mother's head rose again to meet River's eyes. 'Allow me the chance to paint your life, and I promise you; you'll never have to dream again...' he squeezed her hands as he stared down into her eyes.

'You're asking the impossible,' She choked on the words as the hint of a smile turned up the corners of her mouth.

'I'm asking you to marry me,'

'Exactly,' she whispered,

'And what's your answer?'

'Yes,' she beamed as he lifted her into his arms, and she wrapped herself around his neck, his smile buried in her hair as her laugh echoed through his ears.

'You are my one per cent Astraea, and I promise to love you until the last star falls from the sky, and when it does, I'll wish upon it,'

'I'll wish our love will never die,' She finished for him.

I reached out to touch them, as I did, they faded away, and I was back, alone, in the ghost of where they had been, holding the teacup my mother had been holding. 'What happened…?' I breathed out. Twelve years and I had never even known my parents' names; never known what they'd looked like. Sounded like. Now, I had the answers to all of those except, *where were they now?* And *how did we end up here?*

I looked around the abandoned room that was now just scattered with books. I placed the teacup in the sink and started rounding up the lost imaginations of authors long forgotten. I put them on the built-in bookshelf on the back wall and looked up at the array of titles. Then I noticed a gap. There was one missing. I looked around the room. Goldie suddenly perked up and leapt to the end of the sofa expectantly. There under the sofa. I reached down and retrieved a thick bounded book. Goldie followed, sat beside me as I brushed the dust from the cover and read, *The Untold History of Azzurra.* I let the front page fall open, *Written by the collective minds of the Architects.* I sat back and flicked through the pages. They were illustrated, handwritten, and annotated. *Chapter Three: Scions'* I kept flicking through, I saw the five colours we'd learnt in school, including my orange one that had flared up, only once, at the illustrator. On the next page was a drawing of an illustrator and an explanation of how they worked. My mouth dropped open. I held the page open and ran to the bedroom.

I pulled the illustrator from my boot and traced every line of the arched door with the flower painted on it. I reread the page*; once the drawing is complete, the Scion has the ability to bring it to life. Only the Scion that drew the object may possess the object drawn. The object will be made out of the material on which it was drawn.* I closed the book, put the illustrator back in my boot and reached for the handle. I felt the tingle in my fingertips as they went straight through the wall, and the handle came to life in my hand. I felt my hand grip the round doorknob, and with a twist, it clicked open. I let the door fall open. Through the door was the wooden floorboards of a house. I couldn't believe my eyes. My hands shook as I peered inside. 'Hello?' I called out. My

voice echoed through. I placed my hand on the side of

the door. I felt the warmth of the house as my fingers

wrapped around inside. I took a deep breath and stepped

through.

Location: The Sovereign City, River's Home

My footsteps creaked on the old floorboards. The book,

still in my arms, I stepped further through. Goldie crept

at my feet. The house was lit only by side lamps and

candles. 'Hello?' I said a little more quietly as I passed

the doorway to the living room. I stepped inside; it was

small, cosy. Two armchairs, an archway to the next

room. A fireplace in the middle. The flames roared. I felt the heat immediately. I walked over to warm myself. On the mantle were photographs; I reached up and pulled down one that had my parents in. My mum, River and in the middle of them was Selene and *Eos*. My mouth fell open. They knew *both of them*. They were all friends. I closed my eyes and willed a vision, but nothing came. I took the photo from its frame and tried again. Nothing. I sighed and looked around. Another photograph hung on the wall, it was River, and an old man. River's father, maybe… *My Grandfather?* They had the same eyes. I touched the frame. Still, nothing came to me. I stepped back, looked at the book in my hands. I sat on the red, cracked leather chair by the fire and there it was. The ache in my lung that came before the past. It was my mother; she was by the fireplace. She was worried. She sat back into the red leather chair, and I saw the bump of her belly. The door opened and shut; her head flicked towards it. Relief at the sight of Nuri entering. She got to her feet, embraced him.

'What have they decided?' She asked him.

'King Petri ordered for her death the day she's born.' He couldn't even look her in the eye as he spoke. Her lip quivered as she stepped back. She couldn't stand, her hand on her bump; she sat back in the chair, shaking her head.

'No, how could he do this? His own granddaughter.' She looked to Nuri, astonished.

'They're convinced if she lives, war will follow.'

'She is just a child.'

'They're afraid-'

'So, let them be.' She stood up, suddenly outraged. 'Let them fight. Let them know what it is to not be in control.'

'Astraea…' Nuri reached to her, but she batted him away. She began to cry. Her hand to her face, she lowered to her knees as the tears fell. Nuri knelt beside her. She leant into him. Then they were gone. As they faded away, I felt my own cheeks wet with tears.

I sat back into the chair, the book of Azzurra nestled down my side, Goldie curled up on my lap. My parents, wherever they were, had the answers. I had to find them, and I had to do it before anyone could blame them for what happened.

Continued in:

Azzurra;

Duchess of Destruction

Preview

Azzurra;

Duchess of Destruction

12 Years Ago

Location: The Sovereign City, River's Home

It wouldn't be long now. I could hear every tick of the clock. Second, by second, my hope slipped further and further away. I tried not to think about it. Tried to focus my attention on the baby girl in my arms. Sleeping soundly like there wasn't a thing in the world to worry about. My chest tightened at the sound of the front door opening. I felt myself hug Aveline a little bit tighter in my arms. I glanced at the window just a few metres away, a half-step forward, and I stopped myself. The door to the study opened, River. I could barely breathe. His face said it all. He needn't speak. A decision had been made. I felt my head shaking now at his outstretched hand. 'I couldn't change his mind. Your father is adamant. He's sent soldiers.' River's face was solemn as he spoke. Every word poison on his tongue. Tears wavered on my lashes. He didn't hesitate. His arms were around us, holding us close. I held him back, our heads pressed together, looking down at Aveline in my arms. She was so at peace. So innocent. 'It'll be okay,'

'Don't do that. Don't lie to me. Not now.' All of a sudden, I couldn't breathe. 'How do I do this without you?' The words fell from my mouth as I dug my fingers into River's arm. My head shaking. I couldn't process what was happening. Weeks of preparation, of planning but only now had it sunk in what laid ahead. I wasn't ready. I wouldn't ever be ready. I looked at Aveline and then back to him. He held my hand, placed the other on Aveline's blanket-covered chest.

'Until the last star falls.' he said, and instantly I could breathe again. I gave a single nod as salt began to burn my eyes, my chest tightening. I placed my hand over his on Aveline.

'Until the last star falls,' I breathed. The sound of the front door opening. Their footsteps were getting louder, footsteps, more than one person. It was now or never. I looked to the orange chalked drawing of The Sovereign City Gate on the wall across the room as River took a deep calming breath. A single nod between us. I placed my hand around the chalk handle as it came to life at my touch. At the same time, River opened the study door to see CSC soldiers storming towards him. Our eyes met one last time for just a second. I heard him cry out as they knocked him to the side to get through, but we were already gone. A simple chalk outline of our destination left behind.

Location: The Sovereign City, The Pink Mountains

Border

I stood ankle-deep in the icy snow. The Sovereign City

wall standing tall behind me. Aveline in my arms. The

stars twinkling above us. I had no time to waste. I started

forward into the dark abyss ahead of me. It took only

moments for the chill to break through my heavy black

coat. A shiver down my spine. I wrapped my jacket over Aveline to protect her. Suddenly the silence around us broke. A hum from above. My head shot up at the all too familiar sound of a CSC SkySearcher's engine. The sky was clear. No sign of movement. The sound continued to grow. I squinted into the starry sky for its source but nothing. I felt the heat of beaming lights hit us then. I looked down, arm shielding my eyes to see something coming fast towards me across the plane of snow.

I had no escape; in seconds, they were on top of us. The beam turned away as the machine came to a stop, side on to us. I lowered my arm and took in the T-Pod in front of me. My mouth dropped open. It was not a perfect sphere but a slimline, four-seater snowmobile. The awe wore off as the door opened upwards, and my blood began to pulse with adrenaline. I couldn't believe it. Lit up almost into a silhouette from the T-Pod's inner light behind him stood King Petri. 'Dad?' I breathed. I couldn't move. I stood watching as he walked towards me. Towards us. 'How did you find us?'

'Your shoes.' He broke into a smile. I looked down to the thick black boots poking out from beneath my coat. I looked back up at him, confused. 'Bee said they were missing from your wardrobe. You only have one pair of shoes that would survive the Pink Mountains. My heart sank as I sighed out loud. A tear threatening my eyes. I couldn't believe it. I'd planned for so long. Thought of every scenario. 'It's okay,' his voice was soft, comforting as he placed his hand on my shoulder. I realised now he was alone. Not a CSC Solider in sight.

'I don't understand….' The words were barely a whisper as I looked up into my father's crystal blue eyes.

'A father does whatever it takes to protect his children.' He lifted my chin, 'You must believe if there had been, a way, I would've spared her.' He looked down at Aveline. The tear made it to my jaw before it froze in place. He reached into the pocket of his coat and pulled out an Azzurrian Gold coin, and placed it in my hand, wrapping my fingers around it tightly. 'You were always a fighter, Astraea. I knew given no escape, you'd find a way to survive.' He stepped forward, kissed my forehead. 'Tell no one your plan. As cold as the loneliness finds you in the next years, take comfort in knowing that because of you, because of who you've always been, she will always find a helping hand.' He stroked the top of Aveline's head as I fought to keep my tears inside. He started to walk back to the T-Pod.

'Dad.' My voice cracked under the weight of the emotion bearing down on my lungs. He turned back, his face illuminated by the moon's glow.

'Keep my granddaughter safe. Azzurra's going to need her one day. I'm almost certain.' He smiled before turning his back and disappearing into the T-Pod. He didn't hesitate. The snowmobile transformed before my eyes back into the perfect opaque sphere. I stepped aside as it came towards me, heading for the large city gate. I wiped the frozen tears from my cheeks, stuffed the coin deep into my pocket and continued determinedly on into the welcoming darkness of the open snow ahead of us.

Azzurra; The Tale of the Dead Princess

Azzurra; The Tale of the Dead Princess

Printed in Great Britain
by Amazon